VOLPONE; OR, THE FOX

BY
BEN JONSON

Published by Left of Brain Books

Copyright © 2023 Left of Brain Books

ISBN 978-1-396-32452-9

First Edition

PUBLISHER'S PREFACE

About the Book

"Volpone, or The Fox (in Italian: "Big Fox"), is a comedy by Ben Jonson first produced in 1606, drawing on elements of city comedy, black comedy and animal fable. A merciless satire of greed and lust, it remains Jonson's most-performed play, and it is among the finest Jacobean comedies.

Volpone, a Venetian gentleman, is pretending to be on his deathbed after a long illness in order to dupe Voltore, Corbaccio and Corvino, who aspire to his fortune. They each arrive in turn, bearing extravagant gifts with the aim of being inscribed as Volpone's heir. Mosca, Volpone's assistant, encourages them, making each of them believe that he has been named in the will, and getting Corbaccio to disinherit his son in favour of Volpone.

Mosca mentions in passing that Corvino has a beautiful wife, Celia, and Volpone goes to see her in the disguise of Scoto the Mountebank. Corvino drives him away, but Volpone is now insistent that he must have Celia for his own. Mosca tells Corvino that Volpone requires sex with a young woman to help revive him, and will be very grateful to whoever provides the lady. Corvino offers Celia.

Just before Corvino and Celia are due to arrive for this tryst to take place, Corbaccio's son Bonario arrives to catch his father in the act of disinheriting him. Mosca ushers him into a sideroom. Volpone is left alone with Celia, and after failing to seduce her with promises of luxurious items and role-playing fantasies, attempts to rape her. Bonario sees this, comes out of hiding and rescues Celia. However, in the ensuing courtroom sequence, the truth is well-buried by the collusion of Mosca, Volpone and all three of the dupes."

(Quote from wikipedia.org)

About the Author

"Benjamin Jonson (c. 11 June 1572 - 6 August 1637) was an English Renaissance dramatist, poet and actor. A contemporary of William Shakespeare, he is best known for his satirical plays, particularly Volpone and The Alchemist which are considered his best, and his lyric poems. A man of vast reading and a seemingly insatiable appetite for controversy, Jonson had an unparalleled breadth of influence on Jacobean and Caroline playwrights and poets. A house in Dulwich College is named after him."

(Quote from wikipedia.org)

CONTENTS

INTRODUCTION

THE greatest of English dramatists except Shakespeare, the first literary dictator and poet-laureate, a writer of verse, prose, satire, and criticism who most potently of all the men of his time affected the subsequent course of English letters: such was Ben Jonson, and as such his strong personality assumes an interest to us almost unparalleled, at least in his age.

Ben Jonson came of the stock that was centuries after to give to the world Thomas Carlyle; for Jonson's grandfather was of Annandale, over the Solway, whence he migrated to England. Jonson's father lost his estate under Queen Mary, "having been cast into prison and forfeited." He entered the church, but died a month before his illustrious son was born, leaving his widow and child in poverty. Jonson's birthplace was Westminster, and the time of his birth early in 1573. He was thus nearly ten years Shakespeare's junior, and less well off, if a trifle better born. But Jonson did not profit even by this slight advantage. His mother married beneath her, a wright or bricklayer, and Jonson was for a time apprenticed to the trade. As a youth he attracted the attention of the famous antiquary, William Camden, then usher at Westminster School, and there the poet laid the solid foundations of his classical learning. Jonson always held Camden in veneration, acknowledging that to him he owed,

"All that I am in arts, all that I know;" and dedicating his first dramatic success, "Every Man in His Humour," to him. It is doubtful whether Jonson ever went to either university, though Fuller says that he was "statutably admitted into St. John's

College, Cambridge." He tells us that he took no degree, but was later "Master of Arts in both the universities, by their favour, not his study." When a mere youth Jonson enlisted as a soldier, trailing his pike in Flanders in the protracted wars of William the Silent against the Spanish. Jonson was a large and raw-boned lad; he became by his own account in time exceedingly bulky. In chat with his friend William Drummond of Hawthornden, Jonson told how "in his service in the Low Countries he had, in the face of both the camps, killed an enemy, and taken opima spolia from him;" and how "since his coming to England, being appealed to the fields, he had killed his adversary which had hurt him in the arm and whose sword was ten inches longer than his." Jonson's reach may have made up for the lack of his sword; certainly his prowess lost nothing in the telling. Obviously Jonson was brave, combative, and not averse to talking of himself and his doings.

In 1592, Jonson returned from abroad penniless. Soon after he married, almost as early and quite as imprudently as Shakespeare. He told Drummond curtly that "his wife was a shrew, yet honest"; for some years he lived apart from her in the household of Lord Albany. Yet two touching epitaphs among Jonson's "Epigrams," "On my first daughter," and "On my first son," attest the warmth of the poet's family affections. The daughter died in infancy, the son of the plague; another son grew up to manhood little credit to his father whom he survived. We know nothing beyond this of Jonson's domestic life.

How soon Jonson drifted into what we now call grandly "the theatrical profession" we do not know. In 1593, Marlowe made his tragic exit from life, and Greene, Shakespeare's other rival on the popular stage, had preceded Marlowe in an equally miserable death the year before. Shakespeare already had the running to himself. Jonson appears first in the employment of Philip Henslowe, the exploiter of several troupes of players, manager, and father-in-law of the famous actor, Edward Alleyn. From entries in "Henslowe's Diary," a species of theatrical account book which has been handed down to us, we know that Jonson was connected with the Admiral's men; for he borrowed 4 pounds of Henslowe, July 28, 1597, paying back 3s. 9d. on the same day on account of his "share" (in what is not altogether clear); while later, on December 3, of the same year, Henslowe advanced 20s. to him "upon a book which he showed the plot unto the company which he promised to deliver unto the company at Christmas next." In the next August Jonson was in collaboration with Chettle and Porter in a play called "Hot Anger Soon Cold." All this points to an association with Henslowe of some duration, as no mere tyro would be thus paid in advance upon mere promise. From allusions in Dekker's play, "Satiro-mastix," it appears that Jonson, like Shakespeare, began life as an actor, and that he "ambled in a leather pitch by a play-wagon" taking at one time the part of Hieronimo in Kyd's famous play, "The Spanish Tragedy." By the beginning of 1598, Jonson, though still in needy circumstances, had begun to receive recognition. Francis Meres-- well known for his "Comparative Discourse of our English Poets with the Greek, Latin, and Italian Poets," printed in 1598, and for his mention therein of a dozen plays of Shakespeare by title--accords to Ben Jonson a place as one of "our best in tragedy," a matter of some surprise, as no known tragedy of Jonson from so early a date has come down to us. That Jonson was at work on tragedy, however, is proved by the entries in Henslowe of at least three tragedies, now lost, in which he had a hand. These are "Page of Plymouth," "King Robert II. of Scotland," and "Richard Crook-back." But all of these came later, on his return to Henslowe, and range from August 1599 to June 1602.

Returning to the autumn of 1598, an event now happened to sever for a time Jonson's relations with Henslowe. In a letter to

Alleyn, dated September 26 of that year, Henslowe writes: "I have lost one of my company that hurteth me greatly; that is Gabriel *[Spencer],* for he is slain in Hogsden fields by the hands of Benjamin Jonson, bricklayer." The last word is perhaps Henslowe's thrust at Jonson in his displeasure rather than a designation of his actual continuance at his trade up to this time. It is fair to Jonson to remark however, that his adversary appears to have been a notorious fire-eater who had shortly before killed one Feeke in a similar squabble. Duelling was a frequent occurrence of the time among gentlemen and the nobility; it was an impudent breach of the peace on the part of a player. This duel is the one which Jonson described years after to Drummond, and for it Jonson was duly arraigned at Old Bailey, tried, and convicted. He was sent to prison and such goods and chattels as he had "were forfeited." It is a thought to give one pause that, but for the ancient law permitting convicted felons to plead, as it was called, the benefit of clergy, Jonson might have been hanged for this deed. The circumstance that the poet could read and write saved him; and he received only a brand of the letter "T," for Tyburn, on his left thumb. While in jail Jonson became a Roman Catholic; but he returned to the faith of the Church of England a dozen years later.

On his release, in disgrace with Henslowe and his former associates, Jonson offered his services as a playwright to Henslowe's rivals, the Lord Chamberlain's company, in which Shakespeare was a prominent shareholder. A tradition of long standing, though not susceptible of proof in a court of law, narrates that Jonson had submitted the manuscript of "Every Man in His Humour" to the Chamberlain's men and had received from the company a refusal; that Shakespeare called him back, read the play himself, and at once accepted it. Whether this story is true or not, certain it is that "Every Man in His Humour" was accepted by Shakespeare's company and acted for the first time in 1598, with Shakespeare taking a part.

The evidence of this is contained in the list of actors prefixed to the comedy in the folio of Jonson's works, 1616. But it is a mistake to infer, because Shakespeare's name stands first in the list of actors and the elder Kno'well first in the dramatis personae, that Shakespeare took that particular part. The order of a list of Elizabethan players was generally that of their importance or priority as shareholders in the company and seldom if ever corresponded to the list of characters.

"Every Man in His Humour" was an immediate success, and with it Jonson's reputation as one of the leading dramatists of his time was established once and for all. This could have been by no means Jonson's earliest comedy, and we have just learned that he was already reputed one of "our best in tragedy." Indeed, one of Jonson's extant comedies, "The Case is Altered," but one never claimed by him or published as his, must certainly have preceded "Every Man in His Humour" on the stage. The former play may be described as a comedy modelled on the Latin plays of Plautus. (It combines, in fact, situations derived from the "Captivi" and the "Aulularia" of that dramatist). But the pretty story of the beggar-maiden, Rachel, and her suitors, Jonson found, not among the classics, but in the ideals of romantic love which Shakespeare had already popularised on the stage. Jonson never again produced so fresh and lovable a feminine personage as Rachel, although in other respects "The Case is Altered" is not a conspicuous play, and, save for the satirising of Antony Munday in the person of Antonio Balladino and Gabriel Harvey as well, is perhaps the least characteristic of the comedies of Jonson.

"Every Man in His Humour," probably first acted late in the summer of 1598 and at the Curtain, is commonly regarded as an epoch-making play; and this view is not unjustified. As to plot, it tells little more than how an intercepted letter enabled a father to follow his supposedly studious son to London, and there observe his life with the gallants of the time. The real quality of this comedy is in its personages and in the theory upon which they are conceived. Ben Jonson had theories about poetry and the drama, and he was neither chary in talking of them nor in experimenting with them in his plays. This makes Jonson, like Dryden in his time, and Wordsworth much later, an author to reckon with; particularly when we remember that many of Jonson's notions came for a time definitely to prevail and to modify the whole trend of English poetry. First of all Jonson was a classicist, that is, he believed in restraint and precedent in art in opposition to the prevalent ungoverned and irresponsible Renaissance spirit. Jonson believed that there was a profession-al way of doing things which might be reached by a study of the best examples, and he found these examples for the most part among the ancients. To confine our attention to the drama, Jonson objected to the amateurishness and haphazard nature of many contemporary plays, and set himself to do something different; and the first and most striking thing that he evolved was his conception and practice of the comedy of humours.

As Jonson has been much misrepresented in this matter, let us quote his own words as to "humour." A humour, according to Jonson, was a bias of disposition, a warp, so to speak, in character by which

"Some one peculiar quality
Doth so possess a man, that it doth draw
All his affects, his spirits, and his powers,
In their confluctions, all to run one way."

But continuing, Jonson is careful to add:

"But that a rook by wearing a pied feather,
The cable hat-band, or the three-piled ruff,

A yard of shoe-tie, or the Switzers knot
On his French garters, should affect a humour!
O, it is more than most ridiculous."

Jonson's comedy of humours, in a word, conceived of stage personages on the basis of a ruling trait or passion (a notable simplification of actual life be it observed in passing); and, placing these typified traits in juxtaposition in their conflict and contrast, struck the spark of comedy. Downright, as his name indicates, is "a plain squire"; Bobadill's humour is that of the braggart who is incidentally, and with delightfully comic effect, a coward; Brainworm's humour is the finding out of things to the end of fooling everybody: of course he is fooled in the end himself. But it was not Jonson's theories alone that made the success of "Every Man in His Humour." The play is admirably written and each character is vividly conceived, and with a firm touch based on observation of the men of the London of the day. Jonson was neither in this, his first great comedy (nor in any other play that he wrote), a supine classicist, urging that English drama return to a slavish adherence to classical conditions. He says as to the laws of the old comedy (meaning by "laws," such matters as the unities of time and place and the use of chorus): "I see not then, but we should enjoy the same licence, or free power to illustrate and heighten our invention as they *[the ancients]* did; and not be tied to those strict and regular forms which the niceness of a few, who are nothing but form, would thrust upon us." "Every Man in His Humour" is written in prose, a novel practice which Jonson had of his predecessor in comedy, John Lyly. Even the word "humour" seems to have been employed in the Jonsonian sense by Chapman before Jonson's use of it. Indeed, the comedy of humours itself is only a heightened variety of the comedy of manners which represents life, viewed at a satirical angle, and is the oldest and most persistent species of comedy in the language. None the less, Jonson's comedy merited its immediate success and marked out a definite course in which comedy long continued to run. To mention only Shakespeare's Falstaff and his rout, Bardolph, Pistol, Dame Quickly, and the rest, whether in "Henry IV." or in "The Merry Wives of Windsor," all are conceived in the spirit of humours. So are the captains, Welsh, Scotch, and Irish of "Henry V.," and Malvolio especially later; though Shakespeare never employed the method of humours for an important personage. It was not Jonson's fault that many of his successors did precisely the thing that he had reprobated, that is, degrade "the humour: into an oddity of speech, an eccentricity of manner, of dress, or cut of beard. There was an anonymous play called "Every Woman in Her Humour." Chapman wrote "A Humourous Day's Mirth," Day, "Humour Out of Breath," Fletcher later, "The Humourous Lieutenant," and Jonson, besides "Every Man Out of His Humour," returned to the title in closing the cycle of his comedies in "The Magnetic Lady or Humours Reconciled."

With the performance of "Every Man Out of His Humour" in 1599, by Shakespeare's company once more at the Globe, we turn a new page in Jonson's career. Despite his many real virtues, if there is one feature more than any other that distinguishes Jonson, it is his arrogance; and to this may be added his self-righteousness, especially under criticism or satire. "Every Man Out of His Humour" is the first of three "comical satires" which Jonson contributed to what Dekker called the poetomachia or war of the theatres as recent critics have named it. This play as a fabric of plot is a very slight affair; but as a satirical picture of the manners of the time, proceeding by means of vivid caricature, couched in witty and brilliant dialogue and sustained by that righteous indignation which must lie at the heart of all true satire--as a realisation, in short, of the classical ideal of comedy--there had been nothing like Jonson's comedy since the days of Aristophanes. "Every Man in

His Humour," like the two plays that follow it, contains two kinds of attack, the critical or generally satiric, levelled at abuses and corruptions in the abstract; and the personal, in which specific application is made of all this in the lampooning of poets and others, Jonson's contemporaries. The method of personal attack by actual caricature of a person on the stage is almost as old as the drama. Aristophanes so lampooned Euripides in "The Acharnians" and Socrates in "The Clouds," to mention no other examples; and in English drama this kind of thing is alluded to again and again. What Jonson really did, was to raise the dramatic lampoon to an art, and make out of a casual burlesque and bit of mimicry a dramatic satire of literary pretensions and permanency. With the arrogant attitude mentioned above and his uncommon eloquence in scorn, vituperation, and invective, it is no wonder that Jonson soon involved himself in literary and even personal quarrels with his fellow-authors. The circumstances of the origin of this 'poetomachia' are far from clear, and those who have written on the topic, except of late, have not helped to make them clearer. The origin of the "war" has been referred to satirical references, apparently to Jonson, contained in "The Scourge of Villainy," a satire in regular form after the manner of the ancients by John Marston, a fellow playwright, subsequent friend and collaborator of Jonson's. On the other hand, epigrams of Jonson have been discovered (49, 68, and 100) variously charging "playwright" (reasonably identified with Marston) with scurrility, cowardice, and plagiarism; though the dates of the epigrams cannot be ascertained with certainty. Jonson's own statement of the matter to Drummond runs: "He had many quarrels with Marston, beat him, and took his pistol from him, wrote his "Poetaster" on him; the beginning[s] of them were that Marston represented him on the stage." [1]

---

[1] The best account of this whole subject is to be found in the edition of "Poetaster" and "Satiromastrix" by J. H. Penniman in "Belles Lettres

Here at least we are on certain ground; and the principals of the quarrel are known. "Histriomastix," a play revised by Marston in 1598, has been regarded as the one in which Jonson was thus "represented on the stage"; although the personage in question, Chrisogonus, a poet, satirist, and translator, poor but proud, and contemptuous of the common herd, seems rather a complimentary portrait of Jonson than a caricature. As to the personages actually ridiculed in "Every Man Out of His Humour," Carlo Buffone was formerly thought certainly to be Marston, as he was described as "a public, scurrilous, and profane jester," and elsewhere as the grand scourge or second untruss [that is, satirist], of the time" (Joseph Hall being by his own boast the first, and Marston's work being entitled "The Scourge of Villainy"). Apparently we must now prefer for Carlo a notorious character named Charles Chester, of whom gossipy and inaccurate Aubrey relates that he was "a bold impertinent fellow...a perpetual talker and made a noise like a drum in a room. So one time at a tavern Sir Walter Raleigh beats him and seals up his mouth (that is his upper and nether beard) with hard wax. From him Ben Jonson takes his Carlo Buffone ['i.e.', jester] in "Every Man in His Humour" ['sic']." Is it conceivable that after all Jonson was ridiculing Marston, and that the point of the satire consisted in an intentional confusion of "the grand scourge or second untruss" with "the scurrilous and profane" Chester?

We have digressed into detail in this particular case to exemplify the difficulties of criticism in its attempts to identify the allusions in these forgotten quarrels. We are on sounder ground of fact in recording other manifestations of Jonson's enmity. In

---

Series" shortly to appear. See also his earlier work, "The War of the Theatres," 1892, and the excellent contributions to the subject by H. C. Hart in "Notes and Queries," and in his edition of Jonson, 1906.

"The Case is Altered" there is clear ridicule in the character Antonio Balladino of Anthony Munday, pageant-poet of the city, translator of romances and playwright as well. In "Every Man in His Humour" there is certainly a caricature of Samuel Daniel, accepted poet of the court, sonneteer, and companion of men of fashion. These men held recognised positions to which Jonson felt his talents better entitled him; they were hence to him his natural enemies. It seems almost certain that he pursued both in the personages of his satire through "Every Man Out of His Humour," and "Cynthia's Revels," Daniel under the characters Fastidious Brisk and Hedon, Munday as Puntar-volo and Amorphus; but in these last we venture on quagmire once more. Jonson's literary rivalry of Daniel is traceable again and again, in the entertainments that welcomed King James on his way to London, in the masques at court, and in the pastoral drama. As to Jonson's personal ambitions with respect to these two men, it is notable that he became, not pageant-poet, but chronologer to the City of London; and that, on the accession of the new king, he came soon to triumph over Daniel as the accepted entertainer of royalty.

"Cynthia's Revels," the second "comical satire," was acted in 1600, and, as a play, is even more lengthy, elaborate, and impossible than "Every Man Out of His Humour." Here personal satire seems to have absorbed everything, and while much of the caricature is admirable, especially in the detail of witty and trenchantly satirical dialogue, the central idea of a fountain of self-love is not very well carried out, and the persons revert at times to abstractions, the action to allegory. It adds to our wonder that this difficult drama should have been acted by the Children of Queen Elizabeth's Chapel, among them Nathaniel Field with whom Jonson read Horace and Martial, and whom he taught later how to make plays. Another of these precocious little actors was Salathiel Pavy, who died before he was thirteen, already famed for taking the parts of old men. Him Jonson immortalised in one of the sweetest of his epitaphs. An interesting sidelight is this on the character of this redoubtable and rugged satirist, that he should thus have befriended and tenderly remembered these little theatrical waifs, some of whom (as we know) had been literally kidnapped to be pressed into the service of the theatre and whipped to the conning of their difficult parts. To the caricature of Daniel and Munday in "Cynthia's Revels" must be added Anaides (impudence), here assuredly Marston, and Asotus (the prodigal), interpreted as Lodge or, more perilously, Raleigh. Crites, like Asper-Macilente in "Every Man Out of His Humour," is Jonson's self-complaisant portrait of himself, the just, wholly admirable, and judicious scholar, holding his head high above the pack of the yelping curs of envy and detraction, but careless of their puny attacks on his perfections with only too mindful a neglect.

The third and last of the "comical satires" is "Poetaster," acted, once more, by the Children of the Chapel in 1601, and Jonson's only avowed contribution to the fray. According to the author's own account, this play was written in fifteen weeks on a report that his enemies had entrusted to Dekker the preparation of "Satiromastix, the Untrussing of the Humorous Poet," a dramatic attack upon himself. In this attempt to forestall his enemies Jonson succeeded, and "Poetaster" was an immediate and deserved success. While hardly more closely knit in structure than its earlier companion pieces, "Poetaster" is planned to lead up to the ludicrous final scene in which, after a device borrowed from the "Lexiphanes" of Lucian, the offending poetaster, Marston-Crispinus, is made to throw up the difficult words with which he had overburdened his stomach as well as overlarded his vocabulary. In the end Crispinus with his fellow, Dekker-Demetrius, is bound over to keep the peace and never thenceforward "malign, traduce, or detract the person or writings of Quintus Horatius Flaccus *[Jonson]* or any other eminent man transcending you in merit." One of the most diverting personages in Jonson's comedy is Captain Tucca. "His peculiarity" has been well described by Ward as "a buoyant blackguardism which recovers itself instantaneously from the most complete exposure, and a picturesqueness of speech like that of a walking dictionary of slang."

It was this character, Captain Tucca, that Dekker hit upon in his reply, "Satiromastix," and he amplified him, turning his abusive vocabulary back upon Jonson and adding "an immodesty to his dialogue that did not enter into Jonson's conception." It has been held, altogether plausibly, that when Dekker was engaged professionally, so to speak, to write a dramatic reply to Jonson, he was at work on a species of chronicle history, dealing with the story of Walter Terill in the reign of William Rufus. This he hurriedly adapted to include the satirical characters suggested by "Poetaster," and fashioned to convey the satire of his reply. The absurdity of placing Horace in the court of a Norman king is the result. But Dekker's play is not without its palpable hits at the arrogance, the literary pride, and self-righteousness of Jonson-Horace, whose "ningle" or pal, the absurd Asinius Bubo, has recently been shown to figure forth, in all likelihood, Jonson's friend, the poet Drayton. Slight and hastily adapted as is "Satiromastix," especially in a comparison with the better wrought and more significant satire of "Poetaster," the town awarded the palm to Dekker, not to Jonson; and Jonson gave over in consequence his practice of "comical satire." Though Jonson was cited to appear before the Lord Chief Justice to answer certain charges to the effect that he had attacked lawyers and soldiers in "Poetaster," nothing came of this complaint. It may be suspected that much of this furious clatter and give-and-take was pure playing to the gallery. The town was agog with the strife, and on no less an authority than Shakespeare ("Hamlet," ii. 2), we learn that the children's company (acting the plays of Jonson) did "so berattle the common stages...that many, wearing rapiers, are afraid of goose-quills, and dare scarce come thither."

Several other plays have been thought to bear a greater or less part in the war of the theatres. Among them the most important is a college play, entitled "The Return from Parnassus," dating 1601-02. In it a much-quoted passage makes Burbage, as a character, declare: "Why here's our fellow Shakespeare puts them all down; aye and Ben Jonson, too. O that Ben Jonson is a pestilent fellow; he brought up Horace, giving the poets a pill, but our fellow Shakespeare hath given him a purge that made him bewray his credit." Was Shakespeare then concerned in this war of the stages? And what could have been the nature of this "purge"? Among several suggestions, "Troilus and Cressida" has been thought by some to be the play in which Shakespeare thus "put down" his friend, Jonson. A wiser interpretation finds the "purge" in "Satiromastix," which, though not written by Shakespeare, was staged by his company, and therefore with his approval and under his direction as one of the leaders of that company.

The last years of the reign of Elizabeth thus saw Jonson recognised as a dramatist second only to Shakespeare, and not second even to him as a dramatic satirist. But Jonson now turned his talents to new fields. Plays on subjects derived from classical story and myth had held the stage from the beginning of the drama, so that Shakespeare was making no new departure when he wrote his "Julius Caesar" about 1600. Therefore when Jonson staged "Sejanus," three years later and with Shakespeare's company once more, he was only following in the elder dramatist's footsteps. But Jonson's idea of a play on classical history, on the one hand, and Shakespeare's and the elder popular dramatists, on the other, were very different. Heywood some years before had put five straggling plays on the stage in quick succession, all derived from stories in Ovid and dramatised with little taste or discrimination. Shakespeare had a finer conception of form, but even he was contented to take all his ancient history from North's translation of Plutarch and dramatise his subject without further inquiry. Jonson was a scholar and a classical antiquarian. He reprobated this slipshod amateurishness, and wrote his "Sejanus" like a scholar, reading Tacitus, Suetonius, and other authorities, to be certain of his facts, his setting, and his atmosphere, and somewhat pedantically noting his authorities in the margin when he came to print. "Sejanus" is a tragedy of genuine dramatic power in which is told with discriminating taste the story of the haughty favourite of Tiberius with his tragical overthrow. Our drama presents no truer nor more painstaking representation of ancient Roman life than may be found in Jonson's "Sejanus" and "Catiline his Conspiracy," which followed in 1611. A passage in the address of the former play to the reader, in which Jonson refers to a collaboration in an earlier version, has led to the surmise that Shakespeare may have been that "worthier pen." There is no evidence to determine the matter.

In 1605, we find Jonson in active collaboration with Chapman and Marston in the admirable comedy of London life entitled "Eastward Hoe." In the previous year, Marston had dedicated his "Malcontent," in terms of fervid admiration, to Jonson; so that the wounds of the war of the theatres must have been long since healed. Between Jonson and Chapman there was the kinship of similar scholarly ideals. The two continued friends throughout life. "Eastward Hoe" achieved the extraordinary popularity represented in a demand for three issues in one year. But this was not due entirely to the merits of the play. In its earliest version a passage which an irritable courtier conceived to be derogatory to his nation, the Scots, sent both Chapman and Jonson to jail; but the matter was soon patched up, for by this time Jonson had influence at court.

With the accession of King James, Jonson began his long and successful career as a writer of masques. He wrote more masques than all his competitors together, and they are of an extraordinary variety and poetic excellence. Jonson did not invent the masque; for such premeditated devices to set and frame, so to speak, a court ball had been known and practised in varying degrees of elaboration long before his time. But Jonson gave dramatic value to the masque, especially in his invention of the antimasque, a comedy or farcical element of relief, entrusted to professional players or dancers. He enhanced, as well, the beauty and dignity of those portions of the masque in which noble lords and ladies took their parts to create, by their gorgeous costumes and artistic grouping and evolutions, a sumptuous show. On the mechanical and scenic side Jonson had an inventive and ingenious partner in Inigo Jones, the royal architect, who more than any one man raised the standard of stage representation in the England of his day. Jonson continued active in the service of the court in the writing of masques and other entertainments far into the reign of King Charles; but, towards the end, a quarrel with Jones embittered his life, and the two testy old men appear to have become not only a constant irritation to each other, but intolerable bores at court. In "Hymenaei," "The Masque of Queens," "Love Freed from Ignorance," "Lovers made Men," "Pleasure Reconciled to Virtue," and many more will be found Jonson's aptitude, his taste, his poetry and inventiveness in these by-forms of the drama; while in "The Masque of Christmas," and "The Gipsies Metamorphosed" especially, is discoverable that power of broad comedy which, at court as well as in the city, was not the least element of Jonson's contemporary popularity.

But Jonson had by no means given up the popular stage when he turned to the amusement of King James. In 1605 "Volpone" was produced, "The Silent Woman" in 1609, "The Alchemist" in the following year. These comedies, with "Bartholomew Fair," 1614, represent Jonson at his height, and for constructive cleverness, character successfully conceived in the manner of caricature, wit and brilliancy of dialogue, they stand alone in English drama. "Volpone, or the Fox," is, in a sense, a transition play from the dramatic satires of the war of the theatres to the purer comedy represented in the plays named above. Its subject is a struggle of wit applied to chicanery; for among its dramatis personae, from the villainous Fox himself, his rascally servant Mosca, Voltore (the vulture), Corbaccio and Corvino (the big and the little raven), to Sir Politic Would-be and the rest, there is scarcely a virtuous character in the play. Question has been raised as to whether a story so forbidding can be considered a comedy, for, although the plot ends in the discomfiture and imprisonment of the most vicious, it involves no mortal catastrophe. But Jonson was on sound historical ground, for "Volpone" is conceived far more logically on the lines of the ancients' theory of comedy than was ever the romantic drama of Shakespeare, however repulsive we may find a philosophy of life that facilely divides the world into the rogues and their dupes, and, identifying brains with roguery and innocence with folly, admires the former while inconsistently punishing them.

"The Silent Woman" is a gigantic farce of the most ingenious construction. The whole comedy hinges on a huge joke, played by a heartless nephew on his misanthropic uncle, who is induced to take to himself a wife, young, fair, and warranted silent, but who, in the end, turns out neither silent nor a woman at all. In "The Alchemist," again, we have the utmost cleverness in construction, the whole fabric building climax on climax, witty, ingenious, and so plausibly presented that we forget its departures from the possibilities of life. In "The Alchemist" Jonson represented, none the less to the life, certain sharpers of the metropolis, revelling in their shrewdness and rascality and in the variety of the stupidity and wickedness of their victims. We may object to the fact that the only person in the play possessed of a scruple of honesty is discomfited, and that the greatest scoundrel of all is approved in the end and rewarded. The comedy is so admirably written and contrived, the personages stand out with such lifelike distinctness in their several kinds, and the whole is animated with such verve and resourcefulness that "The Alchemist" is a new marvel every time it is read. Lastly of this group comes the tremendous comedy, "Bartholomew Fair," less clear cut, less definite, and less structurally worthy of praise than its three predecessors, but full of the keenest and cleverest of satire and inventive to a degree beyond any English comedy save some other of Jonson's own. It is in "Bartholomew Fair" that we are presented to the immortal caricature of the Puritan, Zeal-in-the-Land Busy, and the Littlewits that group about him, and it is in this extraordi-nary comedy that the humour of Jonson, always open to this danger, loosens into the Rabelaisian mode that so delighted King James in "The Gipsies Metamorphosed." Another comedy of less merit is "The Devil is an Ass," acted in 1616. It was the failure of this play that caused Jonson to give over writing for the public stage for a period of nearly ten years.

"Volpone" was laid as to scene in Venice. Whether because of the success of "Eastward Hoe" or for other reasons, the other three comedies declare in the words of the prologue to "The Alchemist":

"Our scene is London, 'cause we would make known
No country's mirth is better than our own."

Indeed Jonson went further when he came to revise his plays for collected publication in his folio of 1616, he transferred the scene of "Every Man in His Humour" from Florence to London also, converting Signior Lorenzo di Pazzi to Old Kno'well, Prospero to Master Welborn, and Hesperida to Dame Kitely "dwelling i' the Old Jewry."

In his comedies of London life, despite his trend towards caricature, Jonson has shown himself a genuine realist, drawing from the life about him with an experience and insight rare in any generation. A happy comparison has been suggested between Ben Jonson and Charles Dickens. Both were men of the people, lowly born and hardly bred. Each knew the London of his time as few men knew it; and each represented it intimately and in elaborate detail. Both men were at heart moralists, seeking the truth by the exaggerated methods of humour and caricature; perverse, even wrong-headed at times, but possessed of a true pathos and largeness of heart, and when all has been said--though the Elizabethan ran to satire, the Victorian to sentimentality--leaving the world better for the art that they practised in it.

In 1616, the year of the death of Shakespeare, Jonson collected his plays, his poetry, and his masques for publication in a collective edition. This was an unusual thing at the time and had been attempted by no dramatist before Jonson. This volume published, in a carefully revised text, all the plays thus far mentioned, excepting "The Case is Altered," which Jonson did not acknowledge, "Bartholomew Fair," and "The Devil is an Ass," which was written too late. It included likewise a book of some hundred and thirty odd "Epigrams," in which form of brief and pungent writing Jonson was an acknowledged master; "The Forest," a smaller collection of lyric and occasional verse and some ten "Masques" and "Entertainments." In this same year

Jonson was made poet laureate with a pension of one hundred marks a year. This, with his fees and returns from several noblemen, and the small earnings of his plays must have formed the bulk of his income. The poet appears to have done certain literary hack-work for others, as, for example, parts of the Punic Wars contributed to Raleigh's "History of the World." We know from a story, little to the credit of either, that Jonson accompanied Raleigh's son abroad in the capacity of a tutor. In 1618 Jonson was granted the reversion of the office of Master of the Revels, a post for which he was peculiarly fitted; but he did not live to enjoy its perquisites. Jonson was honoured with degrees by both universities, though when and under what circumstances is not known. It has been said that he narrowly escaped the honour of knighthood, which the satirists of the day averred King James was wont to lavish with an indiscriminate hand. Worse men were made knights in his day than worthy Ben Jonson.

From 1616 to the close of the reign of King James, Jonson produced nothing for the stage. But he "prosecuted" what he calls "his wonted studies" with such assiduity that he became in reality, as by report, one of the most learned men of his time. Jonson's theory of authorship involved a wide acquaintance with books and "an ability," as he put it, "to convert the substance or riches of another poet to his own use." Accordingly Jonson read not only the Greek and Latin classics down to the lesser writers, but he acquainted himself especially with the Latin writings of his learned contemporaries, their prose as well as their poetry, their antiquities and curious lore as well as their more solid learning. Though a poor man, Jonson was an indefatigable collector of books. He told Drummond that "the Earl of Pembroke sent him 20 pounds every first day of the new year to buy new books." Unhappily, in 1623, his library was destroyed by fire, an accident serio-comically described in his witty poem, "An Execration upon Vulcan." Yet even now a book turns up from time to time in which is inscribed, in fair large Italian lettering, the name, Ben Jonson. With respect to Jonson's use of his material, Dryden said memorably of him: "*[He]* was not only a professed imitator of Horace, but a learned plagiary of all the others; you track him everywhere in their snow....But he has done his robberies so openly that one sees he fears not to be taxed by any law. He invades authors like a monarch, and what would be theft in other poets is only victory in him." And yet it is but fair to say that Jonson prided himself, and justly, on his originality. In "Catiline," he not only uses Sallust's account of the conspiracy, but he models some of the speeches of Cicero on the Roman orator's actual words. In "Poetaster," he lifts a whole satire out of Horace and dramatises it effectively for his purposes. The sophist Libanius suggests the situation of "The Silent Woman"; a Latin comedy of Giordano Bruno, "Il Cande-laio," the relation of the dupes and the sharpers in "The Alchemist," the "Mostellaria" of Plautus, its admirable opening scene. But Jonson commonly bettered his sources, and putting the stamp of his sovereignty on whatever bullion he borrowed made it thenceforward to all time current and his own.

The lyric and especially the occasional poetry of Jonson has a peculiar merit. His theory demanded design and the perfection of literary finish. He was furthest from the rhapsodist and the careless singer of an idle day; and he believed that Apollo could only be worthily served in singing robes and laurel crowned. And yet many of Jonson's lyrics will live as long as the language. Who does not know "Queen and huntress, chaste and fair." "Drink to me only with thine eyes," or "Still to be neat, still to be dressed"? Beautiful in form, deft and graceful in expression, with not a word too much or one that bears not its part in the total effect, there is yet about the lyrics of Jonson a certain stiffness and formality, a suspicion that they were not quite spontaneous and unbidden, but that they were carved, so to speak, with disproportionate labour by a potent man of letters whose habitual thought is on greater things. It is for these reasons that Jonson is even better in the epigram and in occasional verse where rhetorical finish and pointed wit less interfere with the spontaneity and emotion which we usually associate with lyrical poetry. There are no such epitaphs as Ben Jonson's, witness the charming ones on his own children, on Salathiel Pavy, the child-actor, and many more; and this even though the rigid law of mine and thine must now restore to William Browne of Tavistock the famous lines beginning: "Underneath this sable hearse." Jonson is unsurpassed, too, in the difficult poetry of compliment, seldom falling into fulsome praise and disproportionate similitude, yet showing again and again a generous appreciation of worth in others, a discriminating taste and a generous personal regard. There was no man in England of his rank so well known and universally beloved as Ben Jonson. The list of his friends, of those to whom he had written verses, and those who had written verses to him, includes the name of every man of prominence in the England of King James. And the tone of many of these productions discloses an affectionate familiarity that speaks for the amiable personality and sound worth of the laureate. In 1619, growing unwieldy through inactivity, Jonson hit upon the heroic remedy of a journey afoot to Scotland. On his way thither and back he was hospitably received at the houses of many friends and by those to whom his friends had recommended him. When he arrived in Edinburgh, the burgesses met to grant him the freedom of the city, and Drummond, foremost of Scottish poets, was proud to entertain him for weeks as his guest at Hawthornden. Some of the noblest of Jonson's poems were inspired by friendship. Such is the fine "Ode to the memory of Sir Lucius Cary and Sir Henry Moryson," and that admirable piece of critical insight and filial affection, prefixed to the first Shakespeare folio, "To the memory of my beloved master, William Shakespeare, and what he hath left us," to mention only these.

Nor can the earlier "Epode," beginning "Not to know vice at all," be matched in stately gravity and gnomic wisdom in its own wise and stately age.

But if Jonson had deserted the stage after the publication of his folio and up to the end of the reign of King James, he was far from inactive; for year after year his inexhaustible inventiveness continued to contribute to the masquing and entertainment at court. In "The Golden Age Restored," Pallas turns the Iron Age with its attendant evils into statues which sink out of sight; in "Pleasure Reconciled to Virtue," Atlas figures represented as an old man, his shoulders covered with snow, and Comus, "the god of cheer or the belly," is one of the characters, a circumstance which an imaginative boy of ten, named John Milton, was not to forget. "Pan's Anniversary," late in the reign of James, proclaimed that Jonson had not yet forgotten how to write exquisite lyrics, and "The Gipsies Metamorphosed" displayed the old drollery and broad humorous stroke still unimpaired and unmatchable. These, too, and the earlier years of Charles were the days of the Apollo Room of the Devil Tavern where Jonson presided, the absolute monarch of English literary Bohemia. We hear of a room blazoned about with Jonson's own judicious "Leges Convivales" in letters of gold, of a company made up of the choicest spirits of the time, devotedly attached to their veteran dictator, his reminiscences, opinions, affections, and enmities. And we hear, too, of valorous potations; but in the words of Herrick addressed to his master, Jonson, at the Devil Tavern, as at the Dog, the Triple Tun, and at the Mermaid,

"We such clusters had
As made us nobly wild, not mad,
And yet each verse of thine
Outdid the meat, outdid the frolic wine."

But the patronage of the court failed in the days of King Charles, though Jonson was not without royal favours; and the old poet returned to the stage, producing, between 1625 and 1633, "The Staple of News," "The New Inn," "The Magnetic Lady," and "The Tale of a Tub," the last doubtless revised from a much earlier comedy. None of these plays met with any marked success, although the scathing generalisation of Dryden that designated them "Jonson's dotages" is unfair to their genuine merits. Thus the idea of an office for the gathering, proper dressing, and promulgation of news (wild flight of the fancy in its time) was an excellent subject for satire on the existing absurdities among newsmongers; although as much can hardly be said for "The Magnetic Lady," who, in her bounty, draws to her personages of differing humours to reconcile them in the end according to the alternative title, or "Humours Reconciled." These last plays of the old dramatist revert to caricature and the hard lines of allegory; the moralist is more than ever present, the satire degenerates into personal lampoon, especially of his sometime friend, Inigo Jones, who appears unworthily to have used his influence at court against the broken-down old poet. And now disease claimed Jonson, and he was bedridden for months. He had succeeded Middleton in 1628 as Chronologer to the City of London, but lost the post for not fulfilling its duties. King Charles befriended him, and even commissioned him to write still for the entertainment of the court; and he was not without the sustaining hand of noble patrons and devoted friends among the younger poets who were proud to be "sealed of the tribe of Ben."

Jonson died, August 6, 1637, and a second folio of his works, which he had been some time gathering, was printed in 1640, bearing in its various parts dates ranging from 1630 to 1642. It included all the plays mentioned in the foregoing paragraphs, excepting "The Case is Altered;" the masques, some fifteen, that date between 1617 and 1630; another collection of lyrics and occasional poetry called "Underwoods, including some further entertainments; a translation of "Horace's Art of Poetry" (also published in a vicesimo quarto in 1640), and certain fragments and ingatherings which the poet would hardly have included himself. These last comprise the fragment (less than seventy lines) of a tragedy called "Mortimer his Fall," and three acts of a pastoral drama of much beauty and poetic spirit, "The Sad Shepherd." There is also the exceedingly interesting "English Grammar" "made by Ben Jonson for the benefit of all strangers out of his observation of the English language now spoken and in use," in Latin and English; and "Timber, or Discoveries" "made upon men and matter as they have flowed out of his daily reading, or had their reflux to his peculiar notion of the times." The "Discoveries," as it is usually called, is a commonplace book such as many literary men have kept, in which their reading was chronicled, passages that took their fancy translated or transcribed, and their passing opinions noted. Many passages of Jonson's "Discoveries" are literal translations from the authors he chanced to be reading, with the reference, noted or not, as the accident of the moment prescribed. At times he follows the line of Macchiavelli's argument as to the nature and conduct of princes; at others he clarifies his own conception of poetry and poets by recourse to Aristotle. He finds a choice paragraph on eloquence in Seneca the elder and applies it to his own recollection of Bacon's power as an orator; and another on facile and ready genius, and translates it, adapting it to his recollection of his fellow-playwright, Shakespeare. To call such passages--which Jonson never intended for publication--plagiarism, is to obscure the significance of words. To disparage his memory by citing them is a preposterous use of scholarship. Jonson's prose, both in his dramas, in the descriptive comments of his masques, and in the "Discoveries," is characterised by clarity and vigorous directness, nor is it wanting in a fine sense of form or in the subtler graces of diction.

When Jonson died there was a project for a handsome monument to his memory. But the Civil War was at hand, and the project failed. A memorial, not insufficient, was carved on the stone covering his grave in one of the aisles of Westminster Abbey:

"O rare Ben Jonson."

FELIX E. SCHELLING.

THE COLLEGE,
PHILADELPHIA, U.S.A.

The following is a complete list of his published works:--

DRAMAS:

Every Man in his Humour, 4to, 1601;
The Case is Altered, 4to, 1609;
Every Man out of his Humour, 4to, 1600;
Cynthia's Revels, 4to, 1601;
Poetaster, 4to, 1602;
Sejanus, 4to, 1605;
Eastward Ho (with Chapman and Marston), 4to, 1605;
Volpone, 4to, 1607;
Epicoene, or the Silent Woman, 4to, 1609 (?), fol., 1616;
The Alchemist, 4to, 1612;
Catiline, his Conspiracy, 4to, 1611;
Bartholomew Fayre, 4to, 1614 (?), fol., 1631;
The Divell is an Asse, fol., 1631;
The Staple of Newes, fol., 1631;
The New Sun, 8vo, 1631, fol., 1692;
The Magnetic Lady, or Humours Reconcild, fol., 1640;
A Tale of a Tub, fol., 1640;
The Sad Shepherd, or a Tale of Robin Hood, fol., 1641;

Mortimer his Fall (fragment), fol., 1640.

To Jonson have also been attributed additions to Kyd's Jeronymo, and collaboration in The Widow with Fletcher and Middleton, and in the Bloody Brother with Fletcher.

POEMS:

Epigrams, The Forrest, Underwoods, published in fols., 1616, 1640;
Selections: Execration against Vulcan, and Epigrams, 1640;
G. Hor. Flaccus his art of Poetry, Englished by Ben Jonson, 1640;
Leges Convivialis, fol., 1692.
Other minor poems first appeared in Gifford's edition of Works.

PROSE:
Timber, or Discoveries made upon Men and Matter, fol., 1641;
The English Grammar, made by Ben Jonson for the benefit of Strangers, fol., 1640.

Masques and Entertainments were published in the early folios.

WORKS:

Fol., 1616, volume. 2, 1640 (1631-41);
fol., 1692, 1716-19, 1729;
edited by P. Whalley, 7 volumes., 1756;
by Gifford (with Memoir), 9 volumes., 1816, 1846;
re-edited by F. Cunningham, 3 volumes., 1871;
in 9 volumes., 1875;
by Barry Cornwall (with Memoir), 1838;
by B. Nicholson (Mermaid Series), with Introduction by
C. H. Herford, 1893, etc.;
Nine Plays, 1904;

ed. H. C. Hart (Standard Library), 1906, etc;
Plays and Poems, with Introduction by H. Morley (Universal Library), 1885;
Plays (7) and Poems (Newnes), 1905;
Poems, with Memoir by H. Bennett (Carlton Classics), 1907;
Masques and Entertainments, ed. by H. Morley, 1890.

SELECTIONS:

J. A. Symonds, with Biographical and Critical Essay, (Canterbury Poets), 1886;
Grosart, Brave Translunary Things, 1895;
Arber, Jonson Anthology, 1901;
Underwoods, Cambridge University Press, 1905;
Lyrics (Jonson, Beaumont and Fletcher), the Chap Books, No. 4, 1906;
Songs (from Plays, Masques, etc.), with earliest known setting, Eragny Press, 1906.

LIFE:

See Memoirs affixed to Works;
J. A. Symonds (English Worthies), 1886;
Notes of Ben Jonson Conversations with Drummond of Hawthornden;
Shakespeare Society, 1842;
ed. with Introduction and Notes by P. Sidney, 1906;
Swinburne, A Study of Ben Jonson, 1889.

THE GRATEFUL ACKNOWLEDGER, DEDICATES BOTH IT AND HIMSELF

NEVER, most equal Sisters, had any man a wit so presently excellent, as that it could raise itself; but there must come both matter, occasion, commenders, and favourers to it. If this be true, and that the fortune of all writers doth daily prove it, it behoves the careful to provide well towards these accidents; and, having acquired them, to preserve that part of reputation most tenderly, wherein the benefit of a friend is also defended. Hence is it, that I now render myself grateful, and am studious to justify the bounty of your act; to which, though your mere authority were satisfying, yet it being an age wherein poetry and the professors of it hear so ill on all sides, there will a reason be looked for in the subject. It is certain, nor can it with any forehead be opposed, that the too much license of poetasters in this time, hath much deformed their mistress; that, every day, their manifold and manifest ignorance doth stick unnatural reproaches upon her: but for their petulancy, it were an act of the greatest injustice, either to let the learned suffer, or so divine a skill (which indeed should not be attempted with unclean hands) to fall under the least contempt. For, if men will impartially, and not asquint, look toward the offices and function of a poet, they will easily conclude to themselves the impossibility of any man's being the good poet, without first being a good man. He that is said to be able to inform young men to all good disciplines, inflame grown men to all great virtues, keep old men in their best and supreme state, or, as they decline to childhood, recover them to their first strength; that comes forth the interpreter and arbiter of nature, a teacher of things divine no less than human, a master in manners; and can alone, or with a few, effect the business of mankind: this, I take him, is no subject for pride and ignorance to exercise their railing rhetoric upon. But it will here be hastily answered, that the writers of these days are other things; that not only their manners, but their natures, are inverted, and nothing remaining with them of the dignity of poet, but the abused name, which every scribe usurps; that now, especially in dramatic, or, as they term it, stage-poetry, nothing but ribaldry, profanation, blasphemy, all license of offence to God and man is practised. I dare not deny a great part of this, and am sorry I dare not, because in some men's abortive features (and would they had never boasted the light) it is over-true; but that all are embarked in this bold adventure for hell, is a most uncharitable thought, and, uttered, a more malicious slander. For my particular, I can, and from a most clear conscience, affirm, that I have ever trembled to think toward the least profaneness; have loathed the use of such foul and unwashed bawdry, as is now made the food of the scene: and, howsoever I cannot escape from some, the imputation of sharpness, but that they will say, I have taken a pride, or lust, to be bitter, and not my youngest infant but hath come into the world with all his teeth; I would ask of these supercilious politics, what nation, society, or general order or state, I have provoked? What public person? Whether I have not in all these preserved their dignity, as mine own person, safe? My works are read, allowed, (I speak of those that are intirely mine,) look into them, what broad reproofs have I used? where have I been particular? where personal? except to a mimic, cheater, bawd, or buffoon, creatures, for their insolencies, worthy to be taxed? yet to which of these so pointingly, as he might not either ingenuously have confest, or wisely dissembled his disease? But it is not rumour can make men guilty, much less entitle me to other men's crimes. I know, that nothing can be so innocently writ or carried, but may be made obnoxious to construction; marry, whilst I bear mine innocence about me, I fear it not. Application is now grown a trade with many; and there are that profess to have a key for the decyphering of every thing: but let wise and noble persons take heed how they be too credulous, or give leave to these invading interpreters to be over-familiar with their fames, who cunningly, and often, utter their own virulent malice, under other men's simplest meanings. As for those that will (by faults which charity hath raked up, or common honesty concealed) make themselves a name with the multitude, or, to draw their rude and beastly claps, care not whose living faces they intrench with their petulant styles, may they do it without a rival, for me! I choose rather to live graved in obscurity, than share with them in so preposterous a fame. Nor can I blame the wishes of those severe and wise patriots, who providing the hurts these licentious spirits may do in a state, desire rather to see fools and devils, and those antique relics of barbarism retrieved, with all other ridiculous and exploded follies, than behold the wounds of private men, of princes and nations: for, as Horace makes Trebatius speak among these,

"Sibi quisque timet, quanquam est intactus, et odit."

And men may justly impute such rages, if continued, to the writer, as his sports. The increase of which lust in liberty, together with the present trade of the stage, in all their miscelline interludes, what learned or liberal soul doth not already abhor? where nothing but the filth of the time is uttered, and with such impropriety of phrase, such plenty of solecisms, such dearth of sense, so bold prolepses, so racked metaphors, with brothelry, able to violate the ear of a pagan, and blasphemy, to turn the blood of a Christian to water. I cannot but be serious in a cause of this nature, wherein my fame, and the reputation of divers honest and learned are the question; when a name so full of authority, antiquity, and all great mark, is, through their insolence, become the lowest scorn of the age; and those men subject to the petulancy of every vernaculous orator, that were wont to be the care of kings and happiest monarchs. This it is that hath not only rapt me to present indignation, but made me studious heretofore, and by all my actions, to stand off from them; which may most appear in this my latest work, which you, most learned Arbitresses, have seen, judged, and to my crown, approved; wherein I have laboured for their instruction and amendment, to reduce not only the ancient forms, but manners of the scene, the easiness, the propriety, the innocence, and last, the doctrine, which is the principal end of poesie, to inform men in the best reason of living. And though my catastrophe may, in the strict rigour of comic law, meet with censure, as turning back to my promise; I desire the learned and charitable critic, to have so much faith in me, to think it was done of industry: for, with what ease I could have varied it nearer his scale (but that I fear to boast my own faculty) I could here insert. But my special aim being to put the snaffle in their mouths, that cry out, We never punish vice in our interludes, etc., I took the more liberty; though not without some lines of example, drawn even in the ancients themselves, the goings out of whose comedies are not always joyful, but oft times the bawds, the servants, the rivals, yea, and the masters are mulcted; and fitly, it being the office of a comic poet to imitate justice, and instruct to life, as well as purity of language, or stir up gentle affections; to which I shall take the occasion elsewhere to speak.

For the present, most reverenced Sisters, as I have cared to be thankful for your affections past, and here made the understanding acquainted with some ground of your favours; let me not despair their continuance, to the maturing of some worthier fruits; wherein, if my muses be true to me, I shall raise the despised head of poetry again, and stripping her out of those rotten and base rags wherewith the times have adulterated her form, restore her to her primitive habit, feature, and majesty, and render her worthy to be embraced and kist of all the great and master-spirits of our world. As for the vile and slothful, who never affected an act worthy of celebration, or are so inward with their own vicious natures, as they worthily fear her, and think it an high point of policy to keep her in contempt, with their declamatory and windy invectives; she shall out of just rage incite her servants (who are genus irritabile) to spout ink in their faces, that shall eat farther than their marrow into their fames; and not Cinnamus the barber, with his art, shall be able to take out the brands; but they shall live, and be read, till the wretches die, as things worst deserving of themselves in chief, and then of all mankind.

From my House in the Black-Friars, this 11th day of February, 1607.

PROLOGUE

Now, luck yet sends us, and a little wit
Will serve to make our play hit;
(According to the palates of the season)
Here is rhime, not empty of reason.
This we were bid to credit from our poet,
Whose true scope, if you would know it,
In all his poems still hath been this measure,
To mix profit with your pleasure;
And not as some, whose throats their envy failing,
Cry hoarsely, All he writes is railing:
And when his plays come forth, think they can flout them,
With saying, he was a year about them.
To this there needs no lie, but this his creature,
Which was two months since no feature;
And though he dares give them five lives to mend it,
'Tis known, five weeks fully penn'd it,
From his own hand, without a co-adjutor,
Novice, journey-man, or tutor.
Yet thus much I can give you as a token
Of his play's worth, no eggs are broken,
Nor quaking custards with fierce teeth affrighted,
Wherewith your rout are so delighted;
Nor hales he in a gull old ends reciting,
To stop gaps in his loose writing;
With such a deal of monstrous and forced action,
As might make Bethlem a faction:
Nor made he his play for jests stolen from each table,
But makes jests to fit his fable;
And so presents quick comedy refined,

As best critics have designed;
The laws of time, place, persons he observeth,
From no needful rule he swerveth.
All gall and copperas from his ink he draineth,
Only a little salt remaineth,
Wherewith he'll rub your cheeks, till red, with laughter,
They shall look fresh a week after.

ACT 1.

SCENE 1.1.

A ROOM IN VOLPONE'S HOUSE.

ENTER VOLPONE AND MOSCA.

VOLP:
Good morning to the day; and next, my gold:
Open the shrine, that I may see my Saint.
*[MOSCA WITHDRAWS THE CURTAIN, AND DISCOVERS PILES
OF GOLD, PLATE, JEWELS, ETC.]*
Hail the world's soul, and mine! more glad than is
The teeming earth to see the long'd-for sun
Peep through the horns of the celestial Ram,
Am I, to view thy splendour darkening his;
That lying here, amongst my other hoards,
Shew'st like a flame by night; or like the day
Struck out of chaos, when all darkness fled
Unto the centre. O thou son of Sol,
But brighter than thy father, let me kiss,
With adoration, thee, and every relick
Of sacred treasure, in this blessed room.
Well did wise poets, by thy glorious name,
Title that age which they would have the best;
Thou being the best of things: and far transcending
All style of joy, in children, parents, friends,
Or any other waking dream on earth:
Thy looks when they to Venus did ascribe,
They should have given her twenty thousand Cupids;

Such are thy beauties and our loves! Dear saint,
Riches, the dumb God, that giv'st all men tongues;
That canst do nought, and yet mak'st men do all things;
The price of souls; even hell, with thee to boot,
Is made worth heaven. Thou art virtue, fame,
Honour, and all things else. Who can get thee,
He shall be noble, valiant, honest, wise,--

MOS:

And what he will, sir. Riches are in fortune
A greater good than wisdom is in nature.

VOLP:

True, my beloved Mosca. Yet I glory
More in the cunning purchase of my wealth,
Than in the glad possession; since I gain
No common way; I use no trade, no venture;
I wound no earth with plough-shares; fat no beasts,
To feed the shambles; have no mills for iron,
Oil, corn, or men, to grind them into powder:
I blow no subtle glass; expose no ships
To threat'nings of the furrow-faced sea;
I turn no monies in the public bank,
Nor usure private.

MOS:

No sir, nor devour
Soft prodigals. You shall have some will swallow
A melting heir as glibly as your Dutch
Will pills of butter, and ne'er purge for it;
Tear forth the fathers of poor families
Out of their beds, and coffin them alive
In some kind clasping prison, where their bones
May be forth-coming, when the flesh is rotten:
But your sweet nature doth abhor these courses;
You lothe the widdow's or the orphan's tears
Should wash your pavements, or their piteous cries

Ring in your roofs, and beat the air for vengeance.
VOLP:
Right, Mosca; I do lothe it.
MOS:
And besides, sir,
You are not like a thresher that doth stand
With a huge flail, watching a heap of corn,
And, hungry, dares not taste the smallest grain,
But feeds on mallows, and such bitter herbs;
Nor like the merchant, who hath fill'd his vaults
With Romagnia, and rich Candian wines,
Yet drinks the lees of Lombard's vinegar:
You will not lie in straw, whilst moths and worms
Feed on your sumptuous hangings and soft beds;
You know the use of riches, and dare give now
From that bright heap, to me, your poor observer,
Or to your dwarf, or your hermaphrodite,
Your eunuch, or what other household-trifle
Your pleasure allows maintenance.
VOLP:
Hold thee, Mosca,

[GIVES HIM MONEY.]

Take of my hand; thou strik'st on truth in all,
And they are envious term thee parasite.
Call forth my dwarf, my eunuch, and my fool,
And let them make me sport.

[EXIT MOS.]

What should I do,
But cocker up my genius, and live free
To all delights my fortune calls me to?
I have no wife, no parent, child, ally,

To give my substance to; but whom I make
Must be my heir: and this makes men observe me:
This draws new clients daily, to my house,
Women and men of every sex and age,
That bring me presents, send me plate, coin, jewels,
With hope that when I die (which they expect
Each greedy minute) it shall then return
Ten-fold upon them; whilst some, covetous
Above the rest, seek to engross me whole,
And counter-work the one unto the other,
Contend in gifts, as they would seem in love:
All which I suffer, playing with their hopes,
And am content to coin them into profit,
To look upon their kindness, and take more,
And look on that; still bearing them in hand,
Letting the cherry knock against their lips,
And draw it by their mouths, and back again.--
How now!

[RE-ENTER MOSCA WITH NANO, ANDROGYNO, AND CASTRONE.]

NAN:
Now, room for fresh gamesters, who do will you to know,
They do bring you neither play, nor university show;
And therefore do entreat you, that whatsoever they re-
hearse,
May not fare a whit the worse, for the false pace of the
verse.
If you wonder at this, you will wonder more ere we pass,
For know, here is inclosed the soul of Pythagoras,
That juggler divine, as hereafter shall follow;
Which soul, fast and loose, sir, came first from Apollo,
And was breath'd into Aethalides; Mercurius his son,

Where it had the gift to remember all that ever was done.
From thence it fled forth, and made quick transmigration
To goldy-lock'd Euphorbus, who was killed in good fashion,
At the siege of old Troy, by the cuckold of Sparta.
Hermotimus was next (I find it in my charta)
To whom it did pass, where no sooner it was missing
But with one Pyrrhus of Delos it learn'd to go a fishing;
And thence did it enter the sophist of Greece.
From Pythagore, she went into a beautiful piece,
Hight Aspasia, the meretrix; and the next toss of her
Was again of a whore, she became a philosopher,
Crates the cynick, as it self doth relate it:
Since kings, knights, and beggars, knaves, lords and fools gat it,
Besides, ox and ass, camel, mule, goat, and brock,
In all which it hath spoke, as in the cobler's cock.
But I come not here to discourse of that matter,
Or his one, two, or three, or his greath oath, BY QUATER!
His musics, his trigon, his golden thigh,
Or his telling how elements shift, but I
Would ask, how of late thou best suffered translation,
And shifted thy coat in these days of reformation.

AND:

Like one of the reformed, a fool, as you see,
Counting all old doctrine heresy.

NAN:

But not on thine own forbid meats hast thou ventured?

AND:

On fish, when first a Carthusian I enter'd.

NAN:

Why, then thy dogmatical silence hath left thee?

AND:

Of that an obstreperous lawyer bereft me.

NAN:

O wonderful change, when sir lawyer forsook thee!

For Pythagore's sake, what body then took thee?

AND:

A good dull mule.

NAN:

And how! by that means
Thou wert brought to allow of the eating of beans?

AND:

Yes.

NAN:

But from the mule into whom didst thou pass?

AND:

Into a very strange beast, by some writers call'd an ass;
By others, a precise, pure, illuminate brother,
Of those devour flesh, and sometimes one another;
And will drop you forth a libel, or a sanctified lie,
Betwixt every spoonful of a nativity pie.

NAN:

Now quit thee, for heaven, of that profane nation;
And gently report thy next transmigration.

AND:

To the same that I am.

NAN:

A creature of delight,
And, what is more than a fool, an hermaphrodite!
Now, prithee, sweet soul, in all thy variation,
Which body would'st thou choose, to keep up thy station?

AND:

Troth, this I am in: even here would I tarry.

NAN:

'Cause here the delight of each sex thou canst vary?

AND:

Alas, those pleasures be stale and forsaken;
No, 'tis your fool wherewith I am so taken,
The only one creature that I can call blessed:

For all other forms I have proved most distressed.

NAN:

Spoke true, as thou wert in Pythagoras still.
This learned opinion we celebrate will,
Fellow eunuch, as behoves us, with all our wit and art,
To dignify that whereof ourselves are so great and special a
part.

VOLP:

Now, very, very pretty! Mosca, this
Was thy invention?

MOS:

If it please my patron,
Not else.

VOLP:

It doth, good Mosca.

MOS:

Then it was, sir.
NANO AND CASTRONE *[SING.]:*
Fools, they are the only nation
Worth men's envy, or admiration:
Free from care or sorrow-taking,
Selves and others merry making:
All they speak or do is sterling.
Your fool he is your great man's darling,
And your ladies' sport and pleasure;
Tongue and bauble are his treasure.
E'en his face begetteth laughter,
And he speaks truth free from slaughter;
He's the grace of every feast,
And sometimes the chiefest guest;
Hath his trencher and his stool,
When wit waits upon the fool:
O, who would not be
He, he, he?

[KNOCKING WITHOUT.]

VOLP:
Who's that? Away!

[EXEUNT NANO AND CASTRONE.]

Look, Mosca. Fool, begone!

[EXIT ANDROGYNO.]

MOS:
'Tis Signior Voltore, the advocate;
I know him by his knock.
VOLP:
Fetch me my gown,
My furs and night-caps; say, my couch is changing,
And let him entertain himself awhile
Without i' the gallery.

[EXIT MOSCA.]

Now, now, my clients
Begin their visitation! Vulture, kite,
Raven, and gorcrow, all my birds of prey,
That think me turning carcase, now they come;
I am not for them yet--

[RE-ENTER MOSCA, WITH THE GOWN, ETC.]

How now! the news?
MOS:
A piece of plate, sir.
VOLP:

Of what bigness?

MOS:

Huge,
Massy, and antique, with your name inscribed,
And arms engraven.

VOLP:

Good! and not a fox
Stretch'd on the earth, with fine delusive sleights,
Mocking a gaping crow? ha, Mosca?

MOS:

Sharp, sir.

VOLP:

Give me my furs.

[PUTS ON HIS SICK DRESS.]

Why dost thou laugh so, man?

MOS:

I cannot choose, sir, when I apprehend
What thoughts he has without now, as he walks:
That this might be the last gift he should give;
That this would fetch you; if you died to-day,
And gave him all, what he should be to-morrow;
What large return would come of all his ventures;
How he should worship'd be, and reverenced;
Ride with his furs, and foot-cloths; waited on
By herds of fools, and clients; have clear way
Made for his mule, as letter'd as himself;
Be call'd the great and learned advocate:
And then concludes, there's nought impossible.

VOLP:

Yes, to be learned, Mosca.

MOS:

O no: rich
Implies it. Hood an ass with reverend purple,

So you can hide his two ambitious ears,
And he shall pass for a cathedral doctor.
VOLP:
My caps, my caps, good Mosca. Fetch him in.
MOS:
Stay, sir, your ointment for your eyes.
VOLP:
That's true;
Dispatch, dispatch: I long to have possession
Of my new present.
MOS:
That, and thousands more,
I hope, to see you lord of.
VOLP:
Thanks, kind Mosca.
MOS:
And that, when I am lost in blended dust,
And hundred such as I am, in succession--
VOLP:
Nay, that were too much, Mosca.
MOS:
You shall live,
Still, to delude these harpies.
VOLP:
Loving Mosca!
'Tis well: my pillow now, and let him enter.

[EXIT MOSCA.]

Now, my fain'd cough, my pthisic, and my gout,
My apoplexy, palsy, and catarrhs,
Help, with your forced functions, this my posture,
Wherein, this three year, I have milk'd their hopes.
He comes; I hear him--Uh! *[COUGHING.]* uh! uh! uh! O--

[RE-ENTER MOSCA, INTRODUCING VOLTORE, WITH A PIECE OF PLATE.]

MOS:
> You still are what you were, sir. Only you,
> Of all the rest, are he commands his love,
> And you do wisely to preserve it thus,
> With early visitation, and kind notes
> Of your good meaning to him, which, I know,
> Cannot but come most grateful. Patron! sir!
> Here's signior Voltore is come--

VOLP *[FAINTLY.]:*
> What say you?

MOS:
> Sir, signior Voltore is come this morning
> To visit you.

VOLP:
> I thank him.

MOS:
> And hath brought
> A piece of antique plate, bought of St Mark,
> With which he here presents you.

VOLP:
> He is welcome.
> Pray him to come more often.

MOS:
> Yes.

VOLT:
> What says he?

MOS:
> He thanks you, and desires you see him often.

VOLP:
> Mosca.

MOS:
> My patron!

VOLP:

Bring him near, where is he?
I long to feel his hand.

MOS:

The plate is here, sir.

VOLT:

How fare you, sir?

VOLP:

I thank you, signior Voltore;
Where is the plate? mine eyes are bad.

VOLT *[PUTTING IT INTO HIS HANDS.]:*

I'm sorry,
To see you still thus weak.

MOS *[ASIDE.]:*

That he's not weaker.

VOLP:

You are too munificent.

VOLT:

No sir; would to heaven,
I could as well give health to you, as that plate!

VOLP:

You give, sir, what you can: I thank you. Your love
Hath taste in this, and shall not be unanswer'd:
I pray you see me often.

VOLT:

Yes, I shall sir.

VOLP:

Be not far from me.

MOS:

Do you observe that, sir?

VOLP:

Hearken unto me still; it will concern you.

MOS:

You are a happy man, sir; know your good.

VOLP:

I cannot now last long--

MOS:

You are his heir, sir.

VOLT:

Am I?

VOLP:

I feel me going; Uh! uh! uh! uh!
I'm sailing to my port, Uh! uh! uh! uh!
And I am glad I am so near my haven.

MOS:

Alas, kind gentleman! Well, we must all go--

VOLT:

But, Mosca--

MOS:

Age will conquer.

VOLT:

'Pray thee hear me:
Am I inscribed his heir for certain?

MOS:

Are you!
I do beseech you, sir, you will vouchsafe
To write me in your family. All my hopes
Depend upon your worship: I am lost,
Except the rising sun do shine on me.

VOLT:

It shall both shine, and warm thee, Mosca.

MOS:

Sir,
I am a man, that hath not done your love
All the worst offices: here I wear your keys,
See all your coffers and your caskets lock'd,
Keep the poor inventory of your jewels,
Your plate and monies; am your steward, sir.
Husband your goods here.

VOLT:

But am I sole heir?

MOS:

Without a partner, sir; confirm'd this morning:
The wax is warm yet, and the ink scarce dry
Upon the parchment.

VOLT:

Happy, happy, me!
By what good chance, sweet Mosca?

MOS:

Your desert, sir;
I know no second cause.

VOLT:

Thy modesty
Is not to know it; well, we shall requite it.

MOS:

He ever liked your course sir; that first took him.
I oft have heard him say, how he admired
Men of your large profession, that could speak
To every cause, and things mere contraries,
Till they were hoarse again, yet all be law;
That, with most quick agility, could turn,
And [re-] return; [could] make knots, and undo them;
Give forked counsel; take provoking gold
On either hand, and put it up: these men,
He knew, would thrive with their humility.
And, for his part, he thought he should be blest
To have his heir of such a suffering spirit,
So wise, so grave, of so perplex'd a tongue,
And loud withal, that would not wag, nor scarce
Lie still, without a fee; when every word
Your worship but lets fall, is a chequin!--

[LOUD KNOCKING WITHOUT.]

Who's that? one knocks; I would not have you seen, sir.
And yet--pretend you came, and went in haste:
I'll fashion an excuse.--and, gentle sir,
When you do come to swim in golden lard,
Up to the arms in honey, that your chin
Is born up stiff, with fatness of the flood,
Think on your vassal; but remember me:
I have not been your worst of clients.

VOLT:
Mosca!--

MOS:
When will you have your inventory brought, sir?
Or see a coppy of the will?--Anon!--
I will bring them to you, sir. Away, be gone,
Put business in your face.

[EXIT VOLTORE.]

VOLP *[SPRINGING UP.]:*
Excellent Mosca!
Come hither, let me kiss thee.

MOS:
Keep you still, sir.
Here is Corbaccio.

VOLP:
Set the plate away:
The vulture's gone, and the old raven's come!

MOS:
Betake you to your silence, and your sleep:
Stand there and multiply.

[PUTTING THE PLATE TO THE REST.]

Now, shall we see
A wretch who is indeed more impotent

Than this can feign to be; yet hopes to hop
Over his grave.--

[ENTER CORBACCIO.]

Signior Corbaccio!
You're very welcome, sir.

CORB:

How does your patron?

MOS:

Troth, as he did, sir; no amends.

CORB:

What! mends he?

MOS:

No, sir: he's rather worse.

CORB:

That's well. Where is he?

MOS:

Upon his couch sir, newly fall'n asleep.

CORB:

Does he sleep well?

MOS:

No wink, sir, all this night.
Nor yesterday; but slumbers.

CORB:

Good! he should take
Some counsel of physicians: I have brought him
An opiate here, from mine own doctor.

MOS:

He will not hear of drugs.

CORB:

Why? I myself
Stood by while it was made; saw all the ingredients:
And know, it cannot but most gently work:

My life for his, 'tis but to make him sleep.
VOLP *[ASIDE.]:*

Ay, his last sleep, if he would take it.
MOS:

Sir,

He has no faith in physic.
CORB:

'Say you? 'say you?
MOS:

He has no faith in physic: he does think
Most of your doctors are the greater danger,
And worse disease, to escape. I often have
Heard him protest, that your physician
Should never be his heir.
CORB:

Not I his heir?
MOS:

Not your physician, sir.
CORB:

O, no, no, no,
I do not mean it.
MOS:

No, sir, nor their fees
He cannot brook: he says, they flay a man,
Before they kill him.
CORB:

Right, I do conceive you.
MOS:

And then they do it by experiment;
For which the law not only doth absolve them,
But gives them great reward: and he is loth
To hire his death, so.
CORB:

It is true, they kill,
With as much license as a judge.

MOS:

Nay, more;
For he but kills, sir, where the law condemns,
And these can kill him too.

CORB:

Ay, or me;
Or any man. How does his apoplex?
Is that strong on him still?

MOS:

Most violent.
His speech is broken, and his eyes are set,
His face drawn longer than 'twas wont--

CORB:

How! how!
Stronger then he was wont?

MOS:

No, sir: his face
Drawn longer than 'twas wont.

CORB:

O, good!

MOS:

His mouth
Is ever gaping, and his eyelids hang.

CORB:

Good.

MOS:

A freezing numbness stiffens all his joints,
And makes the colour of his flesh like lead.

CORB:

'Tis good.

MOS:

His pulse beats slow, and dull.

CORB:

Good symptoms, still.

54

MOS:

And from his brain--

CORB:

I conceive you; good.

MOS:

Flows a cold sweat, with a continual rheum,
Forth the resolved corners of his eyes.

CORB:

Is't possible? yet I am better, ha!
How does he, with the swimming of his head?

B:

O, sir, 'tis past the scotomy; he now
Hath lost his feeling, and hath left to snort:
You hardly can perceive him, that he breathes.

CORB:

Excellent, excellent! sure I shall outlast him:
This makes me young again, a score of years.

MOS:

I was a coming for you, sir.

CORB:

Has he made his will?
What has he given me?

MOS:

No, sir.

CORB:

Nothing! ha?

MOS:

He has not made his will, sir.

CORB:

Oh, oh, oh!
But what did Voltore, the Lawyer, here?

MOS:

He smelt a carcase, sir, when he but heard
My master was about his testament;
As I did urge him to it for your good--

CORB:

He came unto him, did he? I thought so.

MOS:

Yes, and presented him this piece of plate.

CORB:

To be his heir?

MOS:

I do not know, sir.

CORB:

True:

I know it too.

MOS

[ASIDE.]:

By your own scale, sir.

CORB:

Well,

I shall prevent him, yet. See, Mosca, look,

Here, I have brought a bag of bright chequines,

Will quite weigh down his plate.

MOS *[TAKING THE BAG.]:*

Yea, marry, sir.

This is true physic, this your sacred medicine,

No talk of opiates, to this great elixir!

CORB:

'Tis aurum palpabile, if not potabile.

MOS:

It shall be minister'd to him, in his bowl.

CORB:

Ay, do, do, do.

MOS:

Most blessed cordial!

This will recover him.

CORB:

Yes, do, do, do.

MOS:

I think it were not best, sir.

CORB:

What?

MOS:

To recover him.

CORB:

O, no, no, no; by no means.

MOS:

Why, sir, this
Will work some strange effect, if he but feel it.

CORB:

'Tis true, therefore forbear; I'll take my venture:
Give me it again.

MOS:

At no hand; pardon me:
You shall not do yourself that wrong, sir. I
Will so advise you, you shall have it all.

CORB:

How?

MOS:

All, sir; 'tis your right, your own; no man
Can claim a part: 'tis yours, without a rival,
Decreed by destiny.

CORB:

How, how, good Mosca?

MOS:

I'll tell you sir. This fit he shall recover.

CORB:

I do conceive you.

MOS:

And, on first advantage
Of his gain'd sense, will I re-importune him
Unto the making of his testament:
And shew him this.

[POINTING TO THE MONEY.]

CORB:

Good, good.

MOS:

'Tis better yet,

If you will hear, sir.

CORB:

Yes, with all my heart.

MOS:

Now, would I counsel you, make home with speed;

There, frame a will; whereto you shall inscribe

My master your sole heir.

CORB:

And disinherit

My son!

MOS:

O, sir, the better: for that colour

Shall make it much more taking.

CORB:

O, but colour?

MOS:

This will sir, you shall send it unto me.

Now, when I come to inforce, as I will do,

Your cares, your watchings, and your many prayers,

Your more than many gifts, your this day's present,

And last, produce your will; where, without thought,

Or least regard, unto your proper issue,

A son so brave, and highly meriting,

The stream of your diverted love hath thrown you

Upon my master, and made him your heir:

He cannot be so stupid, or stone-dead,

But out of conscience, and mere gratitude--

CORB:

He must pronounce me his?

MOS:

'Tis true.

CORB:

This plot
Did I think on before.

MOS:

I do believe it.

CORB:

Do you not believe it?

MOS:

Yes, sir.

CORB:

Mine own project.

MOS:

Which, when he hath done, sir.

CORB:

Publish'd me his heir?

MOS:

And you so certain to survive him--

CORB:

Ay.

MOS:

Being so lusty a man--

CORB:

'Tis true.

MOS:

Yes, sir--

CORB:

I thought on that too. See, how he should be The very organ
to express my thoughts!

MOS:

You have not only done yourself a good--

CORB:

But multiplied it on my son.

MOS:

'Tis right, sir.

CORB:

Still, my invention.

MOS:

'Las, sir! heaven knows,

It hath been all my study, all my care,

(I e'en grow gray withal,) how to work things--

CORB:

I do conceive, sweet Mosca.

MOS:

You are he,

For whom I labour here.

CORB:

Ay, do, do, do:

I'll straight about it.

[GOING.]

MOS:

Rook go with you, raven!

CORB:

I know thee honest.

MOS *[ASIDE.]*:

You do lie, sir!

CORB:

And--

MOS:

Your knowledge is no better than your ears, sir.

CORB:

I do not doubt, to be a father to thee.

MOS:

Nor I to gull my brother of his blessing.

CORB:

I may have my youth restored to me, why not?

MOS:

Your worship is a precious ass!
CORB:
What say'st thou?
MOS:
I do desire your worship to make haste, sir.
CORB:
'Tis done, 'tis done, I go.

[EXIT.]

VOLP *[LEAPING FROM HIS COUCH.]:*
O, I shall burst!
Let out my sides, let out my sides--
MOS:
Contain
Your flux of laughter, sir: you know this hope
Is such a bait, it covers any hook.
VOLP:
O, but thy working, and thy placing it!
I cannot hold; good rascal, let me kiss thee:
I never knew thee in so rare a humour.
MOS:
Alas sir, I but do as I am taught;
Follow your grave instructions; give them words;
Pour oil into their ears, and send them hence.
VOLP:
'Tis true, 'tis true. What a rare punishment
Is avarice to itself!
MOS:
Ay, with our help, sir.
VOLP:
So many cares, so many maladies,
So many fears attending on old age,
Yea, death so often call'd on, as no wish
Can be more frequent with them, their limbs faint,

Their senses dull, their seeing, hearing, going,
All dead before them; yea, their very teeth,
Their instruments of eating, failing them:
Yet this is reckon'd life! nay, here was one;
Is now gone home, that wishes to live longer!
Feels not his gout, nor palsy; feigns himself
Younger by scores of years, flatters his age
With confident belying it, hopes he may,
With charms, like Aeson, have his youth restored:
And with these thoughts so battens, as if fate
Would be as easily cheated on, as he,
And all turns air!

[KNOCKING WITHIN.]

Who's that there, now? a third?
MOS:
Close, to your couch again; I hear his voice:
It is Corvino, our spruce merchant.
VOLP *[LIES DOWN AS BEFORE.]:*
Dead.
MOS:
Another bout, sir, with your eyes.

[ANOINTING THEM.]

--Who's there?

[ENTER CORVINO.]

Signior Corvino! come most wish'd for! O,
How happy were you, if you knew it, now!
CORV:
Why? what? wherein?

MOS:

The tardy hour is come, sir.

CORV:

He is not dead?

MOS:

Not dead, sir, but as good;
He knows no man.

CORV:

How shall I do then?

MOS:

Why, sir?

CORV:

I have brought him here a pearl.

MOS:

Perhaps he has
So much remembrance left, as to know you, sir:
He still calls on you; nothing but your name
Is in his mouth: Is your pearl orient, sir?

CORV:

Venice was never owner of the like.

VOLP *[FAINTLY.]:*

Signior Corvino.

MOS:

Hark.

VOLP:

Signior Corvino!

MOS:

He calls you; step and give it him.--He's here, sir,
And he has brought you a rich pearl.

CORV:

How do you, sir?
Tell him, it doubles the twelfth caract.

MOS:

Sir,
He cannot understand, his hearing's gone;

And yet it comforts him to see you--
CORV:

Say,
I have a diamond for him, too.
MOS:

Best shew it, sir;
Put it into his hand; 'tis only there
He apprehends: he has his feeling, yet.
See how he grasps it!
CORV:

'Las, good gentleman!
How pitiful the sight is!
MOS:

Tut! forget, sir.
The weeping of an heir should still be laughter
Under a visor.
CORV:

Why, am I his heir?
MOS:

Sir, I am sworn, I may not shew the will,
Till he be dead; but, here has been Corbaccio,
Here has been Voltore, here were others too,
I cannot number 'em, they were so many;
All gaping here for legacies: but I,
Taking the vantage of his naming you,
"Signior Corvino, Signior Corvino," took
Paper, and pen, and ink, and there I asked him,
Whom he would have his heir? "Corvino." Who
Should be executor? "Corvino." And,
To any question he was silent too,
I still interpreted the nods he made,
Through weakness, for consent: and sent home th' others,
Nothing bequeath'd them, but to cry and curse.
CORV:

O, my dear Mosca!

[THEY EMBRACE.]

Does he not perceive us?
MOS:
No more than a blind harper. He knows no man,
No face of friend, nor name of any servant,
Who 'twas that fed him last, or gave him drink:
Not those he hath begotten, or brought up,
Can he remember.
CORV:
Has he children?
MOS:
Bastards,
Some dozen, or more, that he begot on beggars,
Gipsies, and Jews, and black-moors, when he was drunk.
Knew you not that, sir? 'tis the common fable.
The dwarf, the fool, the eunuch, are all his;
He's the true father of his family,
In all, save me:--but he has giv'n them nothing.
CORV:
That's well, that's well. Art sure he does not hear us?
MOS:
Sure, sir! why, look you, credit your own sense.

[SHOUTS IN VOL.'S EAR.]

The pox approach, and add to your diseases,
If it would send you hence the sooner, sir,
For your incontinence, it hath deserv'd it
Thoroughly, and thoroughly, and the plague to boot!--
You may come near, sir.--Would you would once close
Those filthy eyes of yours, that flow with slime,
Like two frog-pits; and those same hanging cheeks,

Cover'd with hide, instead of skin--Nay help, sir--
That look like frozen dish-clouts, set on end!

CORV *[ALOUD.]:*

Or like an old smoked wall, on which the rain
Ran down in streaks!

MOS:

Excellent! sir, speak out:
You may be louder yet: A culverin
Discharged in his ear would hardly bore it.

CORV:

His nose is like a common sewer, still running.

MOS:

'Tis good! And what his mouth?

CORV:

A very draught.

MOS:

O, stop it up--

CORV:

By no means.

MOS:

'Pray you, let me.
Faith I could stifle him, rarely with a pillow,
As well as any woman that should keep him.

CORV:

Do as you will: but I'll begone.

MOS:

Be so:
It is your presence makes him last so long.

CORV:

I pray you, use no violence.

MOS:

No, sir! why?
Why should you be thus scrupulous, pray you, sir?

CORV:

Nay, at your discretion.

MOS:

Well, good sir, begone.

CORV:

I will not trouble him now, to take my pearl.

MOS:

Puh! nor your diamond. What a needless care
Is this afflicts you? Is not all here yours?
Am not I here, whom you have made your creature?
That owe my being to you?

CORV:

Grateful Mosca!
Thou art my friend, my fellow, my companion,
My partner, and shalt share in all my fortunes.

MOS:

Excepting one.

CORV:

What's that?

MOS:

Your gallant wife, sir,--

[EXIT CORV.]

Now is he gone: we had no other means
To shoot him hence, but this.

VOLP:

My divine Mosca!
Thou hast to-day outgone thyself.

[KNOCKING WITHIN.]

--Who's there?
I will be troubled with no more. Prepare
Me music, dances, banquets, all delights;
The Turk is not more sensual in his pleasures,

Than will Volpone.

[EXIT MOS.]

Let me see; a pearl!
A diamond! plate! chequines! Good morning's purchase,
Why, this is better than rob churches, yet;
Or fat, by eating, once a month, a man.

[RE-ENTER MOSCA.]

Who is't?
MOS:
The beauteous lady Would-be, sir.
Wife to the English knight, Sir Politick Would-be,
(This is the style, sir, is directed me,)
Hath sent to know how you have slept to-night,
And if you would be visited?
VOLP:
Not now:
Some three hours hence--
MOS:
I told the squire so much.
VOLP:
When I am high with mirth and wine; then, then:
'Fore heaven, I wonder at the desperate valour
Of the bold English, that they dare let loose
Their wives to all encounters!
MOS:
Sir, this knight
Had not his name for nothing, he is politick,
And knows, howe'er his wife affect strange airs,
She hath not yet the face to be dishonest:
But had she signior Corvino's wife's face--

VOLP:

Has she so rare a face?

MOS:

O, sir, the wonder,
The blazing star of Italy! a wench
Of the first year! a beauty ripe as harvest!
Whose skin is whiter than a swan all over,
Than silver, snow, or lilies! a soft lip,
Would tempt you to eternity of kissing!
And flesh that melteth in the touch to blood!
Bright as your gold, and lovely as your gold!

VOLP:

Why had not I known this before?

MOS:

Alas, sir,
Myself but yesterday discover'd it.

VOLP:

How might I see her?

MOS:

O, not possible;
She's kept as warily as is your gold;
Never does come abroad, never takes air,
But at a window. All her looks are sweet,
As the first grapes or cherries, and are watch'd
As near as they are.

VOLP:

I must see her.

MOS:

Sir,
There is a guard of spies ten thick upon her,
All his whole household; each of which is set
Upon his fellow, and have all their charge,
When he goes out, when he comes in, examined.

VOLP:

I will go see her, though but at her window.

MOS:

In some disguise, then.

VOLP:

That is true; I must
Maintain mine own shape still the same: we'll think.

[EXEUNT.]

ACT 2.

SCENE 2.1.

ST. MARK'S PLACE; A RETIRED CORNER BEFORE CORVINO'S HOUSE.

ENTER SIR POLITICK WOULD-BE, AND PEREGRINE.

SIR P:
Sir, to a wise man, all the world's his soil:
It is not Italy, nor France, nor Europe,
That must bound me, if my fates call me forth.
Yet, I protest, it is no salt desire
Of seeing countries, shifting a religion,
Nor any disaffection to the state
Where I was bred, and unto which I owe
My dearest plots, hath brought me out; much less,
That idle, antique, stale, gray-headed project
Of knowing men's minds, and manners, with Ulysses!
But a peculiar humour of my wife's
Laid for this height of Venice, to observe,
To quote, to learn the language, and so forth--
I hope you travel, sir, with license?

PER:
Yes.

SIR P:
I dare the safelier converse--How long, sir,
Since you left England?

PER:
Seven weeks.

SIR P:

So lately!
You have not been with my lord ambassador?

PER:

Not yet, sir.

SIR P:

Pray you, what news, sir, vents our climate?
I heard last night a most strange thing reported
By some of my lord's followers, and I long
To hear how 'twill be seconded.

PER:

What was't, sir?

SIR P:

Marry, sir, of a raven that should build
In a ship royal of the king's.

PER

[ASIDE.]:
This fellow,
Does he gull me, trow? or is gull'd?
--Your name, sir.

SIR P:

My name is Politick Would-be.

PER

[ASIDE.]:
O, that speaks him.
--A knight, sir?

SIR P:

A poor knight, sir.

PER:

Your lady
Lies here in Venice, for intelligence
Of tires, and fashions, and behaviour,
Among the courtezans? the fine lady Would-be?

SIR P:

Yes, sir; the spider and the bee, ofttimes,
Suck from one flower.

PER:

Good Sir Politick,
I cry you mercy; I have heard much of you:
'Tis true, sir, of your raven.

SIR P:

On your knowledge?

PER:

Yes, and your lion's whelping, in the Tower.

SIR P:

Another whelp!

PER:

Another, sir.

SIR P:

Now heaven!
What prodigies be these? The fires at Berwick!
And the new star! these things concurring, strange,
And full of omen! Saw you those meteors?

PER:

I did, sir.

SIR P:

Fearful! Pray you, sir, confirm me,
Were there three porpoises seen above the bridge,
As they give out?

PER:

Six, and a sturgeon, sir.

SIR P:

I am astonish'd.

PER:

Nay, sir, be not so;
I'll tell you a greater prodigy than these.

SIR P:

What should these things portend?

PER:

The very day
(Let me be sure) that I put forth from London,
There was a whale discover'd in the river,
As high as Woolwich, that had waited there,
Few know how many months, for the subversion
Of the Stode fleet.

SIR P:

Is't possible? believe it,
'Twas either sent from Spain, or the archdukes:
Spinola's whale, upon my life, my credit!
Will they not leave these projects? Worthy sir,
Some other news.

PER:

Faith, Stone the fool is dead;
And they do lack a tavern fool extremely.

SIR P:

Is Mass Stone dead?

PER:

He's dead sir; why, I hope
You thought him not immortal?
[ASIDE.]
--O, this knight,
Were he well known, would be a precious thing
To fit our English stage: he that should write
But such a fellow, should be thought to feign
Extremely, if not maliciously.

SIR P:

Stone dead!

PER:

Dead.--Lord! how deeply sir, you apprehend it?
He was no kinsman to you?

SIR P:

That I know of.
Well! that same fellow was an unknown fool.

PER:

And yet you knew him, it seems?

SIR P:

I did so. Sir,

I knew him one of the most dangerous heads

Living within the state, and so I held him.

PER:

Indeed, sir?

SIR P:

While he lived, in action.

He has received weekly intelligence,

Upon my knowledge, out of the Low Countries,

For all parts of the world, in cabbages;

And those dispensed again to ambassadors,

In oranges, musk-melons, apricocks,

Lemons, pome-citrons, and such-like: sometimes

In Colchester oysters, and your Selsey cockles.

PER:

You make me wonder.

SIR P:

Sir, upon my knowledge.

Nay, I've observed him, at your public ordinary,

Take his advertisement from a traveller

A conceal'd statesman, in a trencher of meat;

And instantly, before the meal was done,

Convey an answer in a tooth-pick.

PER:

Strange!

How could this be, sir?

SIR P:

Why, the meat was cut

So like his character, and so laid, as he

Must easily read the cipher.

PER:

I have heard,

He could not read, sir.
SIR P:
So 'twas given out,
In policy, by those that did employ him:
But he could read, and had your languages,
And to't, as sound a noddle--
PER:
I have heard, sir,
That your baboons were spies, and that they were
A kind of subtle nation near to China:
SIR P:
Ay, ay, your Mamuluchi. Faith, they had
Their hand in a French plot or two; but they
Were so extremely given to women, as
They made discovery of all: yet I
Had my advices here, on Wednesday last.
From one of their own coat, they were return'd,
Made their relations, as the fashion is,
And now stand fair for fresh employment.
PER:
'Heart!

[ASIDE.]

This sir Pol will be ignorant of nothing.
--It seems, sir, you know all?
SIR P:
Not all sir, but
I have some general notions. I do love
To note and to observe: though I live out,
Free from the active torrent, yet I'd mark
The currents and the passages of things,
For mine own private use; and know the ebbs,
And flows of state.

PER:

Believe it, sir, I hold
Myself in no small tie unto my fortunes,
For casting me thus luckily upon you,
Whose knowledge, if your bounty equal it,
May do me great assistance, in instruction
For my behaviour, and my bearing, which
Is yet so rude and raw.

SIR P:

Why, came you forth
Empty of rules, for travel?

PER:

Faith, I had
Some common ones, from out that vulgar grammar,
Which he that cried Italian to me, taught me.

SIR P:

Why this it is, that spoils all our brave bloods,
Trusting our hopeful gentry unto pedants,
Fellows of outside, and mere bark. You seem
To be a gentleman, of ingenuous race:--
I not profess it, but my fate hath been
To be, where I have been consulted with,
In this high kind, touching some great men's sons,
Persons of blood, and honour.--

*[ENTER MOSCA AND NANO DISGUISED, FOLLOWED BY PERSONS
WITH MATERIALS FOR ERECTING A STAGE.]*

PER:

Who be these, sir?

MOS:

Under that window, there 't must be. The same.

SIR P:

Fellows, to mount a bank. Did your instructor
In the dear tongues, never discourse to you

Of the Italian mountebanks?

PER:

Yes, sir.

SIR P:

Why,
Here shall you see one.

PER:

They are quacksalvers;
Fellows, that live by venting oils and drugs.

SIR P:

Was that the character he gave you of them?

PER:

As I remember.

SIR P:

Pity his ignorance.
They are the only knowing men of Europe!
Great general scholars, excellent physicians,
Most admired statesmen, profest favourites,
And cabinet counsellors to the greatest princes;
The only languaged men of all the world!

PER:

And, I have heard, they are most lewd impostors;
Made all of terms and shreds; no less beliers
Of great men's favours, than their own vile med'cines;
Which they will utter upon monstrous oaths:
Selling that drug for two-pence, ere they part,
Which they have valued at twelve crowns before.

SIR P:

Sir, calumnies are answer'd best with silence.
Yourself shall judge.--Who is it mounts, my friends?

MOS:

Scoto of Mantua, sir.

SIR P:

Is't he? Nay, then

I'll proudly promise, sir, you shall behold
Another man than has been phant'sied to you.
I wonder yet, that he should mount his bank,
Here in this nook, that has been wont t'appear
In face of the Piazza!--Here, he comes.

[ENTER VOLPONE, DISGUISED AS A MOUNTEBANK DOCTOR, AND FOLLOWED BY A CROWD OF PEOPLE.]

VOLP *[TO NANO.]*:
Mount zany.
MOB:
Follow, follow, follow, follow!
SIR P:
See how the people follow him! he's a man
May write ten thousand crowns in bank here. Note,

[VOLPONE MOUNTS THE STAGE.]

Mark but his gesture:--I do use to observe
The state he keeps in getting up.
PER:
'Tis worth it, sir.
VOLP:
Most noble gentlemen, and my worthy patrons! It may seem strange, that I, your Scoto Mantuano, who was ever wont to fix my bank in face of the public Piazza, near the shelter of the Portico to the Procuratia, should now, after eight months' absence from this illustrious city of Venice, humbly retire myself into an obscure nook of the Piazza.
SIR P:
Did not I now object the same?
PER:
Peace, sir.
VOLP:

Let me tell you: I am not, as your Lombard proverb saith, cold on my feet; or content to part with my commodities at a cheaper rate, than I accustomed: look not for it. Nor that the calumnious reports of that impudent detractor, and shame to our profession, (Alessandro Buttone, I mean,) who gave out, in public, I was condemn'd a sforzato to the galleys, for poisoning the cardinal Bembo's--cook, hath at all attached, much less dejected me. No, no, worthy gentlemen; to tell you true, I cannot endure to see the rabble of these ground ciarlitani, that spread their cloaks on the pavement, as if they meant to do feats of activity, and then come in lamely, with their mouldy tales out of Boccacio, like stale Tabarine, the fabulist: some of them discoursing their travels, and of their tedious captivity in the Turks' galleys, when, indeed, were the truth known, they were the Christians' galleys, where very temperately they eat bread, and drunk water, as a wholesome penance, enjoined them by their confessors, for base pilferies.

SIR P:

Note but his bearing, and contempt of these.

VOLP:

These turdy-facy-nasty-paty-lousy-fartical rogues, with one poor groat's-worth of unprepared antimony, finely wrapt up in several scartoccios, are able, very well, to kill their twenty a week, and play; yet, these meagre, starved spirits, who have half stopt the organs of their minds with earthy oppilations, want not their favourers among your shrivell'd sallad-eating artizans, who are overjoyed that they may have their half-pe'rth of physic; though it purge them into another world, it makes no matter.

SIR P:

Excellent! have you heard better language, sir?

VOLP:

Well, let them go. And, gentlemen, honourable gentlemen, know, that for this time, our bank, being thus removed from the clamours of the canaglia, shall be the scene of pleasure and delight; for I have nothing to sell, little or nothing to sell.

SIR P:

I told you, sir, his end.

PER:

You did so, sir.

VOLP:

I protest, I, and my six servants, are not able to make of this precious liquor, so fast as it is fetch'd away from my lodging by gentlemen of your city; strangers of the Terra-firma; worshipful merchants; ay, and senators too: who, ever since my arrival, have detained me to their uses, by their splendidous liberalities. And worthily; for, what avails your rich man to have his magazines stuft with moscadelli, or of the purest grape, when his physicians prescribe him, on pain of death, to drink nothing but water cocted with aniseeds? O health! health! the blessing of the rich, the riches of the poor! who can buy thee at too dear a rate, since there is no enjoying this world without thee? Be not then so sparing of your purses, honourable gentlemen, as to abridge the natural course of life--

PER:

You see his end.

SIR P:

Ay, is't not good?

VOLP:

For, when a humid flux, or catarrh, by the mutability of air, falls from your head into an arm or shoulder, or any other part; take you a ducat, or your chequin of gold, and apply to the place affected: see what good effect it can work. No, no, 'tis this blessed unguento, this rare extraction, that hath only power to disperse all malignant humours, that proceed either of hot, cold, moist, or windy causes--

PER:

I would he had put in dry too.

SIR P:

'Pray you, observe.

VOLP:

To fortify the most indigest and crude stomach, ay, were it of one, that, through extreme weakness, vomited blood, applying only a warm napkin to the place, after the unction and fricace;--for the vertigine in the head, putting but a drop into your nostrils, likewise behind the ears; a most sovereign and approved remedy. The mal caduco, cramps, convulsions, paralysies, epilepsies, tremor-cordia, retired nerves, ill vapours of the spleen, stopping of the liver, the stone, the strangury, hernia ventosa, iliaca passio; stops a disenteria immediately; easeth the torsion of the small guts: and cures melancholia hypocondriaca, being taken and applied according to my printed receipt. *[POINTING TO HIS BILL AND HIS VIAL.]* For, this is the physician, this the medicine; this counsels, this cures; this gives the direction, this works the effect; and, in sum, both together may be termed an abstract of the theorick and practick in the Aesculapian art. 'Twill cost you eight crowns. And,--Zan Fritada, prithee sing a verse extempore in honour of it.

SIR P:

How do you like him, sir?

PER:

Most strangely, I!

SIR P:

Is not his language rare?

PER:

But alchemy,
I never heard the like: or Broughton's books.

NANO *[SINGS.]:*

Had old Hippocrates, or Galen,
That to their books put med'cines all in,
But known this secret, they had never
(Of which they will be guilty ever)
Been murderers of so much paper,
Or wasted many a hurtless taper;
No Indian drug had e'er been famed,
Tabacco, sassafras not named;
Ne yet, of guacum one small stick, sir,
Nor Raymund Lully's great elixir.
Ne had been known the Danish Gonswart,
Or Paracelsus, with his long-sword.

PER:

All this, yet, will not do, eight crowns is high.

VOLP:

No more.--Gentlemen, if I had but time to discourse to you the miraculous effects of this my oil, surnamed Oglio del Scoto; with the countless catalogue of those I have cured of the aforesaid, and many more diseases; the pattents and privileges of all the princes and commonwealths of Christendom; or but the depositions of those that appeared on my part, before the signiory of the Sanita and most learned College of Physicians; where I was authorised, upon notice taken of the admirable virtues of my medicaments, and mine own excellency in matter of rare and unknown secrets, not only to disperse them publicly in this famous city, but in all the territories, that happily joy under the government of the most pious and magnificent states of Italy. But may some other gallant fellow say, O, there be divers that make profession to have as good, and as experimented receipts as yours: indeed, very many have assayed, like apes, in imitation of that, which is really and essentially in me, to make of this oil; bestowed great cost in furnaces, stills, alembecks, continual fires, and preparation of the ingredients, (as indeed there goes to it six hundred several simples, besides some quantity of human fat, for the conglutination, which we buy of the anatomists,) but, when these practitioners come to the last decoction, blow, blow, puff, puff, and all flies in fumo: ha, ha, ha! Poor wretches! I rather pity their folly and indiscretion, than their loss of time and money; for these may be recovered by industry: but to be a fool born, is a disease incurable. For myself, I always from my youth have endeavoured to get the rarest secrets, and book them, either in exchange, or for money; I spared nor cost nor labour, where any thing was worthy to be learned. And gentlemen, honourable gentlemen, I will undertake, by virtue of chemical art, out of the honourable hat that covers your head, to extract the four elements; that is to say, the fire, air, water, and earth, and return you your felt without burn or stain. For, whilst others have been at the Balloo, I have been at my book; and am now past the craggy paths of study, and come to the flowery plains of honour and reputation.

SIR P:

I do assure you, sir, that is his aim.

VOLP:

But, to our price--

PER:

And that withal, sir Pol.

VOLP:

You all know, honourable gentlemen, I never valued this ampulla, or vial, at less than eight crowns, but for this time, I am content, to be deprived of it for six; six crowns is the price; and less, in courtesy I know you cannot offer me; take it, or leave it, howsoever, both it and I am at your service. I ask you not as the value of the thing, for then I should demand of you a thousand crowns, so the cardinals Montalto, Fernese, the great Duke of Tuscany, my gossip, with divers other princes, have given me; but I despise money. Only to shew my affection to you, honourable gentlemen, and your illustrious State here, I have neglected the messages of these princes, mine own offices, framed my journey hither, only to present you with the fruits of my travels.--Tune your voices once more to the touch of your instruments, and give the honourable assembly some delightful recreation.

PER:

What monstrous and most painful circumstance
Is here, to get some three or four gazettes,
Some three-pence in the whole! for that 'twill come to.

NANO *[SINGS.]:*

You that would last long, list to my song,
Make no more coil, but buy of this oil.
Would you be ever fair and young?
Stout of teeth, and strong of tongue?
Tart of palate? quick of ear?
Sharp of sight? of nostril clear?
Moist of hand? and light of foot?
Or, I will come nearer to't,
Would you live free from all diseases?
Do the act your mistress pleases;
Yet fright all aches from your bones?
Here's a med'cine, for the nones.

VOLP:

Well, I am in a humour at this time to make a present of the small quantity my coffer contains; to the rich, in courtesy, and to the poor for God's sake. Wherefore now mark: I ask'd you six crowns, and six crowns, at other times, you have paid me; you shall not give me six crowns, nor five, nor four, nor three, nor two, nor one; nor half a ducat; no, nor a moccinigo. Sixpence it will cost you, or six hundred pound-- expect no lower price, for, by the banner of my front, I will not bate a bagatine, that I will have, only, a pledge of your loves, to carry something from amongst you, to shew I am

not contemn'd by you. Therefore, now, toss your handker-
chiefs, cheerfully, cheerfully; and be advertised, that the
first heroic spirit that deignes to grace me with a handkerchief, I will give it a little remembrance of something, beside, shall please it better, than if I had presented it with a
double pistolet.

PER:

Will you be that heroic spark, sir Pol?

*[CELIA AT A WINDOW ABOVE, THROWS DOWN HER
HANDKERCHIEF.]*

O see! the window has prevented you.

VOLP:

Lady, I kiss your bounty; and for this timely grace you have
done your poor Scoto of Mantua, I will return you, over and
above my oil, a secret of that high and inestimable nature,
shall make you for ever enamour'd on that minute, wherein
your eye first descended on so mean, yet not altogether to
be despised, an object. Here is a powder conceal'd in this
paper, of which, if I should speak to the worth, nine thousand volumes were but as one page, that page as a line, that
line as a word; so short is this pilgrimage of man (which
some call life) to the expressing of it. Would I reflect on the
price? why, the whole world is but as an empire, that empire as a province, that province as a bank, that bank as a
private purse to the purchase of it. I will only tell you; it is
the powder that made Venus a goddess (given her by Apollo,) that kept her perpetually young, clear'd her wrinkles,
firm'd her gums, fill'd her skin, colour'd her hair; from her
deriv'd to Helen, and at the sack of Troy unfortunately lost:
till now, in this our age, it was as happily recovered, by a
studious antiquary, out of some ruins of Asia, who sent a
moiety of it to the court of France, (but much sophisti-

cated,) wherewith the ladies there, now, colour their hair. The rest, at this present, remains with me; extracted to a quintessence: so that, whereever it but touches, in youth it perpetually preserves, in age restores the complexion; seats your teeth, did they dance like virginal jacks, firm as a wall; makes them white as ivory, that were black, as--

[ENTER CORVINO.]

COR:
Spight o' the devil, and my shame! come down here;
Come down;--No house but mine to make your scene?
Signior Flaminio, will you down, sir? down?
What, is my wife your Franciscina, sir?
No windows on the whole Piazza, here,
To make your properties, but mine? but mine?

[BEATS AWAY VOLPONE, NANO, ETC.]

Heart! ere to-morrow, I shall be new-christen'd,
And call'd the Pantalone di Besogniosi,
About the town.
PER:
What should this mean, sir Pol?
SIR P:
Some trick of state, believe it. I will home.
PER:
It may be some design on you:
SIR P:
I know not.
I'll stand upon my guard.
PER:
It is your best, sir.
SIR P:
This three weeks, all my advices, all my letters,

They have been intercepted.

PER:

Indeed, sir!

Best have a care.

SIR P:

Nay, so I will.

PER: This knight,

I may not lose him, for my mirth, till night.

[EXEUNT.]

SCENE 2.2.

A ROOM IN VOLPONE'S HOUSE.

ENTER VOLPONE AND MOSCA.

VOLP:

O, I am wounded!

MOS:

Where, sir?

VOLP:

Not without;

Those blows were nothing: I could bear them ever.

But angry Cupid, bolting from her eyes,

Hath shot himself into me like a flame;

Where, now, he flings about his burning heat,

As in a furnace an ambitious fire,

Whose vent is stopt. The fight is all within me.

I cannot live, except thou help me, Mosca;

My liver melts, and I, without the hope

Of some soft air, from her refreshing breath,

Am but a heap of cinders.

MOS:

'Las, good sir,
Would you had never seen her!
VOLP:
Nay, would thou
Had'st never told me of her!
MOS:
Sir 'tis true;
I do confess I was unfortunate,
And you unhappy: but I'm bound in conscience,
No less than duty, to effect my best
To your release of torment, and I will, sir.
VOLP:
Dear Mosca, shall I hope?
MOS:
Sir, more than dear,
I will not bid you to dispair of aught
Within a human compass.
VOLP:
O, there spoke
My better angel. Mosca, take my keys,
Gold, plate, and jewels, all's at thy devotion;
Employ them how thou wilt; nay, coin me too:
So thou, in this, but crown my longings, Mosca.
MOS:
Use but your patience.
VOLP:
So I have.
MOS:
I doubt not
To bring success to your desires.
VOLP:
Nay, then,
I not repent me of my late disguise.
MOS:
If you can horn him, sir, you need not.

VOLP:

True:
Besides, I never meant him for my heir.--
Is not the colour of my beard and eyebrows,
To make me known?

MOS:

No jot.

VOLP:

I did it well.

MOS:

So well, would I could follow you in mine,
With half the happiness!

[ASIDE.]

--and yet I would
Escape your Epilogue.

VOLP:

But were they gull'd
With a belief that I was Scoto?

MOS:

Sir,
Scoto himself could hardly have distinguish'd!
I have not time to flatter you now; we'll part;
And as I prosper, so applaud my art.

[EXEUNT.]

SCENE 2.3.

A ROOM IN CORVINO'S HOUSE.

ENTER CORVINO, WITH HIS SWORD IN HIS HAND, DRAGGING IN CELIA.

CORV:

> Death of mine honour, with the city's fool!
> A juggling, tooth-drawing, prating mountebank!
> And at a public window! where, whilst he,
> With his strain'd action, and his dole of faces,
> To his drug-lecture draws your itching ears,
> A crew of old, unmarried, noted letchers,
> Stood leering up like satyrs; and you smile
> Most graciously, and fan your favours forth,
> To give your hot spectators satisfaction!
> What; was your mountebank their call? their whistle?
> Or were you enamour'd on his copper rings,
> His saffron jewel, with the toad-stone in't,
> Or his embroider'd suit, with the cope-stitch,
> Made of a herse-cloth? or his old tilt-feather?
> Or his starch'd beard? Well; you shall have him, yes!
> He shall come home, and minister unto you
> The fricace for the mother. Or, let me see,
> I think you'd rather mount; would you not mount?
> Why, if you'll mount, you may; yes truly, you may:
> And so you may be seen, down to the foot.
> Get you a cittern, lady Vanity,
> And be a dealer with the virtuous man;
> Make one: I'll but protest myself a cuckold,
> And save your dowry. I'm a Dutchman, I!
> For, if you thought me an Italian,
> You would be damn'd, ere you did this, you whore!
> Thou'dst tremble, to imagine, that the murder
> Of father, mother, brother, all thy race,
> Should follow, as the subject of my justice.

CEL:

> Good sir, have pacience.

CORV:

> What couldst thou propose
> Less to thyself, than in this heat of wrath

    And stung with my dishonour, I should strike
    This steel into thee, with as many stabs,
    As thou wert gaz'd upon with goatish eyes?

CEL:

    Alas, sir, be appeas'd! I could not think
    My being at the window should more now
    Move your impatience, than at other times.

CORV:

    No! not to seek and entertain a parley
    With a known knave, before a multitude!
    You were an actor with your handkerchief;
    Which he most sweetly kist in the receipt,
    And might, no doubt, return it with a letter,
    And point the place where you might meet: your sister's,
    Your mother's, or your aunt's might serve the turn.

CEL:

    Why, dear sir, when do I make these excuses,
    Or ever stir abroad, but to the church?
    And that so seldom--

CORV:

    Well, it shall be less;
    And thy restraint before was liberty,
    To what I now decree: and therefore mark me.
    First, I will have this bawdy light damm'd up;
    And till't be done, some two or three yards off,
    I'll chalk a line: o'er which if thou but chance
    To set thy desperate foot; more hell, more horror
    More wild remorseless rage shall seize on thee,
    Than on a conjurer, that had heedless left
    His circle's safety ere his devil was laid.
    Then here's a lock which I will hang upon thee;
    And, now I think on't, I will keep thee backwards;
    Thy lodging shall be backwards; thy walks backwards;
    Thy prospect, all be backwards; and no pleasure,

That thou shalt know but backwards: nay, since you force
My honest nature, know, it is your own,
Being too open, makes me use you thus:
Since you will not contain your subtle nostrils
In a sweet room, but they must snuff the air
Of rank and sweaty passengers.

[KNOCKING WITHIN.]

--One knocks.
Away, and be not seen, pain of thy life;
Nor look toward the window: if thou dost--
Nay, stay, hear this--let me not prosper, whore,
But I will make thee an anatomy,
Dissect thee mine own self, and read a lecture
Upon thee to the city, and in public.
Away!

[EXIT CELIA.]

[ENTER SERVANT.]

Who's there?
SERV:
'Tis signior Mosca, sir.
CORV:
Let him come in.

[EXIT SERVANT.]

His master's dead: There's yet
Some good to help the bad.--

[ENTER MOSCA.]

My Mosca, welcome!
I guess your news.
MOS:

I fear you cannot, sir.
CORV:

Is't not his death?
MOS:

Rather the contrary.
CORV:

Not his recovery?
MOS:

Yes, sir,
CORV:

I am curs'd,
I am bewitch'd, my crosses meet to vex me.
How? how? how? how?
MOS:

Why, sir, with Scoto's oil;
Corbaccio and Voltore brought of it,
Whilst I was busy in an inner room--
CORV:

Death! that damn'd mountebank; but for the law
Now, I could kill the rascal: it cannot be,
His oil should have that virtue. Have not I
Known him a common rogue, come fidling in
To the osteria, with a tumbling whore,
And, when he has done all his forced tricks, been glad
Of a poor spoonful of dead wine, with flies in't?
It cannot be. All his ingredients
Are a sheep's gall, a roasted bitch's marrow,
Some few sod earwigs pounded caterpillars,
A little capon's grease, and fasting spittle:
I know them to a dram.
MOS:

I know not, sir,
But some on't, there, they pour'd into his ears,
Some in his nostrils, and recover'd him;
Applying but the fricace.

CORV:

Pox o' that fricace.

MOS:

And since, to seem the more officious
And flatt'ring of his health, there, they have had,
At extreme fees, the college of physicians
Consulting on him, how they might restore him;
Where one would have a cataplasm of spices,
Another a flay'd ape clapp'd to his breast,
A third would have it a dog, a fourth an oil,
With wild cats' skins: at last, they all resolved
That, to preserve him, was no other means,
But some young woman must be straight sought out,
Lusty, and full of juice, to sleep by him;
And to this service, most unhappily,
And most unwillingly, am I now employ'd,
Which here I thought to pre-acquaint you with,
For your advice, since it concerns you most;
Because, I would not do that thing might cross
Your ends, on whom I have my whole dependance, sir:
Yet, if I do it not, they may delate
My slackness to my patron, work me out
Of his opinion; and there all your hopes,
Ventures, or whatsoever, are all frustrate!
I do but tell you, sir. Besides, they are all
Now striving, who shall first present him; therefore--
I could entreat you, briefly conclude somewhat;
Prevent them if you can.

CORV:

Death to my hopes,
This is my villainous fortune! Best to hire

Some common courtezan.

MOS:

Ay, I thought on that, sir;
But they are all so subtle, full of art--
And age again doting and flexible,
So as--I cannot tell--we may, perchance,
Light on a quean may cheat us all.

CORV:

'Tis true.

MOS:

No, no: it must be one that has no tricks, sir,
Some simple thing, a creature made unto it;
Some wench you may command. Have you no kinswoman?
Odso--Think, think, think, think, think, think, think, sir.
One o' the doctors offer'd there his daughter.

CORV:

How!

MOS:

Yes, signior Lupo, the physician.

CORV:

His daughter!

MOS:

And a virgin, sir. Why? alas,
He knows the state of's body, what it is;
That nought can warm his blood sir, but a fever;
Nor any incantation raise his spirit:
A long forgetfulness hath seized that part.
Besides sir, who shall know it? some one or two--

CORV:

I prithee give me leave.

[WALKS ASIDE.]

If any man

But I had had this luck--The thing in't self,
I know, is nothing--Wherefore should not I
As well command my blood and my affections,
As this dull doctor? In the point of honour,
The cases are all one of wife and daughter.

MOS *[ASIDE.]:*

I hear him coming.

CORV:

She shall do't: 'tis done.
Slight! if this doctor, who is not engaged,
Unless 't be for his counsel, which is nothing,
Offer his daughter, what should I, that am
So deeply in? I will prevent him: Wretch!
Covetous wretch!--Mosca, I have determined.

MOS:

How, sir?

CORV:

We'll make all sure. The party you wot of
Shall be mine own wife, Mosca.

MOS:

Sir, the thing,
But that I would not seem to counsel you,
I should have motion'd to you, at the first:
And make your count, you have cut all their throats.
Why! 'tis directly taking a possession!
And in his next fit, we may let him go.
'Tis but to pull the pillow from his head,
And he is throttled: it had been done before,
But for your scrupulous doubts.

CORV:

Ay, a plague on't, My conscience fools my wit! Well, I'll be
brief, And so be thou, lest they should be before us: Go
home, prepare him, tell him with what zeal And willingness I
do it; swear it was On the first hearing, as thou mayst do,
truly, Mine own free motion.

MOS: Sir, I warrant you,
I'll so possess him with it, that the rest
Of his starv'd clients shall be banish'd all;
And only you received. But come not, sir,
Until I send, for I have something else
To ripen for your good, you must not know't.

CORV:

But do not you forget to send now.

MOS:

Fear not.

[EXIT.]

CORV:

Where are you, wife? my Celia? wife?

[RE-ENTER CELIA.]

--What, blubbering?
Come, dry those tears. I think thou thought'st me in earn-
est;
Ha! by this light I talk'd so but to try thee:
Methinks the lightness of the occasion
Should have confirm'd thee. Come, I am not jealous.

CEL:

No!

CORV:

Faith I am not I, nor never was;
It is a poor unprofitable humour.
Do not I know, if women have a will,
They'll do 'gainst all the watches of the world,
And that the feircest spies are tamed with gold?
Tut, I am confident in thee, thou shalt see't;
And see I'll give thee cause too, to believe it.

Come kiss me. Go, and make thee ready, straight,
In all thy best attire, thy choicest jewels,
Put them all on, and, with them, thy best looks:
We are invited to a solemn feast,
At old Volpone's, where it shall appear
How far I am free from jealousy or fear.

[exeunt.]

ACT 3.

SCENE 3.1.

A STREET.

ENTER MOSCA.

MOS:
I fear, I shall begin to grow in love
With my dear self, and my most prosperous parts,
They do so spring and burgeon; I can feel
A whimsy in my blood: I know not how,
Success hath made me wanton. I could skip
Out of my skin, now, like a subtle snake,
I am so limber. O! your parasite
Is a most precious thing, dropt from above,
Not bred 'mongst clods, and clodpoles, here on earth.
I muse, the mystery was not made a science,
It is so liberally profest! almost
All the wise world is little else, in nature,
But parasites, or sub-parasites.--And yet,
I mean not those that have your bare town-art,
To know who's fit to feed them; have no house,
No family, no care, and therefore mould
Tales for men's ears, to bait that sense; or get
Kitchen-invention, and some stale receipts
To please the belly, and the groin; nor those,
With their court dog-tricks, that can fawn and fleer,
Make their revenue out of legs and faces,
Echo my lord, and lick away a moth:

But your fine elegant rascal, that can rise,
And stoop, almost together, like an arrow;
Shoot through the air as nimbly as a star;
Turn short as doth a swallow; and be here,
And there, and here, and yonder, all at once;
Present to any humour, all occasion;
And change a visor, swifter than a thought!
This is the creature had the art born with him;
Toils not to learn it, but doth practise it
Out of most excellent nature: and such sparks
Are the true parasites, others but their zanis.

[ENTER BONARIO.]

MOS:

Who's this? Bonario, old Corbaccio's son?
The person I was bound to seek.--Fair sir,
You are happily met.

BON:

That cannot be by thee.

MOS:

Why, sir?

BON:

Nay, pray thee know thy way, and leave me:
I would be loth to interchange discourse
With such a mate as thou art

MOS:

Courteous sir,
Scorn not my poverty.

BON:

Not I, by heaven;
But thou shalt give me leave to hate thy baseness.

MOS:

Baseness!

BON:

Ay; answer me, is not thy sloth
Sufficient argument? thy flattery?
Thy means of feeding?

MOS:
Heaven be good to me!
These imputations are too common, sir,
And easily stuck on virtue when she's poor.
You are unequal to me, and however,
Your sentence may be righteous, yet you are not
That, ere you know me, thus proceed in censure:
St. Mark bear witness 'gainst you, 'tis inhuman.

[WEEPS.]

BON *[ASIDE.]:*
What! does he weep? the sign is soft and good;
I do repent me that I was so harsh.

MOS:
'Tis true, that, sway'd by strong necessity,
I am enforced to eat my careful bread
With too much obsequy; 'tis true, beside,
That I am fain to spin mine own poor raiment
Out of my mere observance, being not born
To a free fortune: but that I have done
Base offices, in rending friends asunder,
Dividing families, betraying counsels,
Whispering false lies, or mining men with praises,
Train'd their credulity with perjuries,
Corrupted chastity, or am in love
With mine own tender ease, but would not rather
Prove the most rugged, and laborious course,
That might redeem my present estimation,
Let me here perish, in all hope of goodness.

BON *[ASIDE.]:*

This cannot be a personated passion.--
I was to blame, so to mistake thy nature;
Prithee, forgive me: and speak out thy business.
MOS:
Sir, it concerns you; and though I may seem,
At first to make a main offence in manners,
And in my gratitude unto my master;
Yet, for the pure love, which I bear all right,
And hatred of the wrong, I must reveal it.
This very hour your father is in purpose
To disinherit you--
BON:
How!
MOS:
And thrust you forth,
As a mere stranger to his blood; 'tis true, sir:
The work no way engageth me, but, as
I claim an interest in the general state
Of goodness and true virtue, which I hear
To abound in you: and, for which mere respect,
Without a second aim, sir, I have done it.
BON:
This tale hath lost thee much of the late trust
Thou hadst with me; it is impossible:
I know not how to lend it any thought,
My father should be so unnatural.
MOS:
It is a confidence that well becomes
Your piety; and form'd, no doubt, it is
From your own simple innocence: which makes
Your wrong more monstrous, and abhorr'd. But, sir,
I now will tell you more. This very minute,
It is, or will be doing; and, if you
Shall be but pleas'd to go with me, I'll bring you,
I dare not say where you shall see, but where

Your ear shall be a witness of the deed;
Hear yourself written bastard; and profest
The common issue of the earth.

BON:

I am amazed!

MOS:

Sir, if I do it not, draw your just sword,
And score your vengeance on my front and face;
Mark me your villain: you have too much wrong,
And I do suffer for you, sir. My heart
Weeps blood in anguish--

BON:

Lead; I follow thee.

[EXEUNT.]

SCENE 3.2.

A ROOM IN VOLPONE'S HOUSE.

ENTER VOLPONE.

VOLP:

Mosca stays long, methinks. Bring forth your sports,
And help to make the wretched time more sweet.

[ENTER NANO, ANDROGYNO, AND CASTRONE.]

NAN:

Dwarf, fool, and eunuch, well met here we be.
A question it were now, whether of us three,
Being all the known delicates of a rich man,
In pleasing him, claim the precedency can?

CAS:

>I claim for myself.
AND:
>And so doth the fool.
NAN:
>'Tis foolish indeed: let me set you both to school.
>First for your dwarf, he's little and witty,
>And every thing, as it is little, is pretty;
>Else why do men say to a creature of my shape,
>So soon as they see him, It's a pretty little ape?
>And why a pretty ape, but for pleasing imitation
>Of greater men's actions, in a ridiculous fashion?
>Beside, this feat body of mine doth not crave
>Half the meat, drink, and cloth, one of your bulks will have.
>Admit your fool's face be the mother of laughter,
>Yet, for his brain, it must always come after:
>And though that do feed him, 'tis a pitiful case,
>His body is beholding to such a bad face.

[KNOCKING WITHIN.]

VOLP:
>Who's there? my couch; away! look! Nano, see:

[EXE. AND. AND CAS.]

>Give me my caps, first--go, enquire.

[EXIT NANO.]

>--Now, Cupid
>Send it be Mosca, and with fair return!
NAN *[WITHIN.]*:
>It is the beauteous madam--
VOLP:
>Would-be?--is it?

NAN:
> The same.

VOLP:
> Now torment on me! Squire her in;
> For she will enter, or dwell here for ever:
> Nay, quickly.

[RETIRES TO HIS COUCH.]

> --That my fit were past! I fear
> A second hell too, that my lothing this
> Will quite expel my appetite to the other:
> Would she were taking now her tedious leave.
> Lord, how it threats me what I am to suffer!

[RE-ENTER NANO, WITH LADY POLITICK WOULD-BE.]

LADY P:
> I thank you, good sir. 'Pray you signify
> Unto your patron, I am here.--This band
> Shews not my neck enough.--I trouble you, sir;
> Let me request you, bid one of my women
> Come hither to me.--In good faith, I, am drest
> Most favorably, to-day! It is no matter:
> 'Tis well enough.--

[ENTER 1 WAITING-WOMAN.]

> Look, see, these petulant things,
> How they have done this!

VOLP *[ASIDE.]*:
> I do feel the fever
> Entering in at mine ears; O, for a charm,
> To fright it hence.

LADY P:

>Come nearer: Is this curl
>In his right place, or this? Why is this higher
>Then all the rest? You have not wash'd your eyes, yet!
>Or do they not stand even in your head?
>Where is your fellow? call her.

[EXIT 1 WOMAN.]

NAN:

>Now, St. Mark
>Deliver us! anon, she will beat her women,
>Because her nose is red.

[RE-ENTER 1 WITH 2 WOMAN.]

LADY P:

>I pray you, view
>This tire, forsooth; are all things apt, or no?

1 WOM:

>One hair a little, here, sticks out, forsooth.

LADY P:

>Does't so, forsooth? and where was your dear sight,
>When it did so, forsooth! What now! bird-eyed?
>And you too? 'Pray you, both approach and mend it.
>Now, by that light, I muse you are not ashamed!
>I, that have preach'd these things so oft unto you,
>Read you the principles, argued all the grounds,
>Disputed every fitness, every grace,
>Call'd you to counsel of so frequent dressings--

NAN *[ASIDE.]:*

>More carefully than of your fame or honour.

LADY P:

>Made you acquainted, what an ample dowry
>The knowledge of these things would be unto you,

Able, alone, to get you noble husbands
At your return: and you thus to neglect it!
Besides you seeing what a curious nation
The Italians are, what will they say of me?
"The English lady cannot dress herself."
Here's a fine imputation to our country:
Well, go your ways, and stay, in the next room.
This fucus was too course too, it's no matter.--
Good-sir, you will give them entertainment?

[EXEUNT NANO AND WAITING-WOMEN.]

VOLP:

The storm comes toward me.
LADY P *[GOES TO THE COUCH.]*:

How does my Volpone?
VOLP:

Troubled with noise, I cannot sleep; I dreamt
That a strange fury enter'd, now, my house,
And, with the dreadful tempest of her breath,
Did cleave my roof asunder.
LADY P:

Believe me, and I
Had the most fearful dream, could I remember't--
VOLP *[ASIDE.]*:

Out on my fate! I have given her the occasion
How to torment me: she will tell me hers.
LADY P:

Me thought, the golden mediocrity,
Polite and delicate--
VOLP:

O, if you do love me,
No more; I sweat, and suffer, at the mention
Of any dream: feel, how I tremble yet.

LADY P:

Alas, good soul! the passion of the heart.
Seed-pearl were good now, boil'd with syrup of apples,
Tincture of gold, and coral, citron-pills,
Your elicampane root, myrobalanes--

VOLP *[ASIDE.]:*

Ah me, I have ta'en a grass-hopper by the wing!

LADY P:

Burnt silk, and amber: you have muscadel
Good in the house--

VOLP:

You will not drink, and part?

LADY P:

No, fear not that. I doubt, we shall not get
Some English saffron, half a dram would serve;
Your sixteen cloves, a little musk, dried mints,
Bugloss, and barley-meal--

VOLP *[ASIDE.]:*

She's in again!
Before I fain'd diseases, now I have one.

LADY P:

And these applied with a right scarlet cloth.

VOLP *[ASIDE.]:*

Another flood of words! a very torrent!

LADY P:

Shall I, sir, make you a poultice?

VOLP:

No, no, no;
I am very well: you need prescribe no more.

LADY P:

I have a little studied physic; but now,
I'm all for music, save, in the forenoons,
An hour or two for painting. I would have
A lady, indeed, to have all, letters, and arts,
Be able to discourse, to write, to paint,

But principal, as Plato holds, your music,
And, so does wise Pythagoras, I take it,
Is your true rapture: when there is concent
In face, in voice, and clothes: and is, indeed,
Our sex's chiefest ornament.

VOLP:
The poet
As old in time as Plato, and as knowing,
Says that your highest female grace is silence.

LADY P:
Which of your poets? Petrarch, or Tasso, or Dante?
Guarini? Ariosto? Aretine?
Cieco di Hadria? I have read them all.

VOLP *[ASIDE.]:*
Is every thing a cause to my distruction?

LADY P:
I think I have two or three of them about me.

VOLP *[ASIDE.]:*
The sun, the sea will sooner both stand still,
Then her eternal tongue; nothing can 'scape it.

LADY P:
Here's pastor Fido--

VOLP *[ASIDE.]:*
Profess obstinate silence,
That's now my safest.

LADY P:
All our English writers,
I mean such as are happy in the Italian,
Will deign to steal out of this author, mainly:
Almost as much, as from Montagnie;
He has so modern and facile a vein,
Fitting the time, and catching the court-ear!
Your Petrarch is more passionate, yet he,
In days of sonetting, trusted them with much:

Dante is hard, and few can understand him.
But, for a desperate wit, there's Aretine;
Only, his pictures are a little obscene--
You mark me not.
VOLP:
Alas, my mind is perturb'd.
LADY P:
Why, in such cases, we must cure ourselves,
Make use of our philosophy--
VOLP:
Oh me!
LADY P:
And as we find our passions do rebel,
Encounter them with reason, or divert them,
By giving scope unto some other humour
Of lesser danger: as, in politic bodies,
There's nothing more doth overwhelm the judgment,
And cloud the understanding, than too much
Settling and fixing, and, as 'twere, subsiding
Upon one object. For the incorporating
Of these same outward things, into that part,
Which we call mental, leaves some certain faeces
That stop the organs, and as Plato says,
Assassinate our Knowledge.
VOLP *[ASIDE.]:*
Now, the spirit
Of patience help me!
LADY P:
Come, in faith, I must
Visit you more a days; and make you well:
Laugh and be lusty.
VOLP *[ASIDE.]:*
My good angel save me!
LADY P:
There was but one sole man in all the world,

With whom I e'er could sympathise; and he
Would lie you, often, three, four hours together
To hear me speak; and be sometimes so rapt,
As he would answer me quite from the purpose,
Like you, and you are like him, just. I'll discourse,
An't be but only, sir, to bring you asleep,
How we did spend our time and loves together,
For some six years.
VOLP:
Oh, oh, oh, oh, oh, oh!
LADY P:
For we were coaetanei, and brought up--
VOLP:
Some power, some fate, some fortune rescue me!

[ENTER MOSCA.]

MOS:
God save you, madam!
LADY P:
Good sir.
VOLP:
Mosca? welcome,
Welcome to my redemption.
MOS:
Why, sir?
VOLP:
Oh,
Rid me of this my torture, quickly, there;
My madam, with the everlasting voice:
The bells, in time of pestilence, ne'er made
Like noise, or were in that perpetual motion!
The Cock-pit comes not near it. All my house,
But now, steam'd like a bath with her thick breath.

A lawyer could not have been heard; nor scarce
Another woman, such a hail of words
She has let fall. For hell's sake, rid her hence.

MOS:

Has she presented?

VOLP:

O, I do not care;
I'll take her absence, upon any price,
With any loss.

MOS:

Madam--

LADY P:

I have brought your patron
A toy, a cap here, of mine own work.

MOS:

'Tis well.
I had forgot to tell you, I saw your knight,
Where you would little think it.--

LADY P:

Where?

MOS:

Marry,
Where yet, if you make haste, you may apprehend,
Rowing upon the water in a gondole,
With the most cunning courtezan of Venice.

LADY P:

Is't true?

MOS:

Pursue them, and believe your eyes;
Leave me, to make your gift.

[EXIT LADY P. HASTILY.]

--I knew 'twould take:
For, lightly, they, that use themselves most license,

Are still most jealous.

VOLP:

Mosca, hearty thanks,
For thy quick fiction, and delivery of me.
Now to my hopes, what say'st thou?

[RE-ENTER LADY P. WOULD-BE.]

LADY P:

But do you hear, sir?--

VOLP:

Again! I fear a paroxysm.

LADY P:

Which way
Row'd they together?

MOS:

Toward the Rialto.

LADY P:

I pray you lend me your dwarf.

MOS:

I pray you, take him.--

[EXIT LADY P.]

Your hopes, sir, are like happy blossoms, fair,
And promise timely fruit, if you will stay
But the maturing; keep you at your couch,
Corbaccio will arrive straight, with the Will;
When he is gone, I'll tell you more.

[EXIT.]

VOLP:

My blood,

My spirits are return'd; I am alive:
And like your wanton gamester, at primero,
Whose thought had whisper'd to him, not go less,
Methinks I lie, and draw--for an encounter.

[THE SCENE CLOSES UPON VOLPONE.]

SCENE 3.3

THE PASSAGE LEADING TO VOLPONE'S CHAMBER.

ENTER MOSCA AND BONARIO.

MOS:
Sir, here conceal'd,

[SHEWS HIM A CLOSET.]

you may here all. But, pray you,
Have patience, sir;

[KNOCKING WITHIN.]

--the same's your father knocks:
I am compell'd to leave you.

[EXIT.]

BON:
Do so.--Yet,
Cannot my thought imagine this a truth.

[GOES INTO THE CLOSET.]

SCENE 3.4.

ANOTHER PART OF THE SAME.

ENTER MOSCA AND CORVINO, CELIA FOLLOWING.

MOS:
Death on me! you are come too soon, what meant you?
Did not I say, I would send?
CORV:
Yes, but I fear'd
You might forget it, and then they prevent us.
MOS *[ASIDE.]:*
Prevent! did e'er man haste so, for his horns?
A courtier would not ply it so, for a place.
--Well, now there's no helping it, stay here;
I'll presently return.

[EXIT.]

CORV:
Where are you, Celia?
You know not wherefore I have brought you hither?
CEL:
Not well, except you told me.
CORV:
Now, I will:
Hark hither.

[EXEUNT.]

SCENE 3.5.

A CLOSET OPENING INTO A GALLERY.

ENTER MOSCA AND BONARIO.

MOS:

Sir, your father hath sent word,
It will be half an hour ere he come;
And therefore, if you please to walk the while
Into that gallery--at the upper end,
There are some books to entertain the time:
And I'll take care no man shall come unto you, sir.

BON:

Yes, I will stay there.
[ASIDE.]--I do doubt this fellow.

[EXIT.]

MOS [LOOKING AFTER HIM.]:

There; he is far enough;
he can hear nothing:
And, for his father, I can keep him off.

[EXIT.]

SCENE 3.6.

VOLPONE'S CHAMBER.--VOLPONE ON HIS COUCH. MOSCA SITTING BY HIM.

ENTER CORVINO, FORCING IN CELIA.

CORV:

Nay, now, there is no starting back, and therefore,
Resolve upon it: I have so decreed.
It must be done. Nor would I move't, afore,
Because I would avoid all shifts and tricks,
That might deny me.

CEL:

Sir, let me beseech you,

Affect not these strange trials; if you doubt
My chastity, why, lock me up for ever:
Make me the heir of darkness. Let me live,
Where I may please your fears, if not your trust.

CORV:

Believe it, I have no such humour, I.
All that I speak I mean; yet I'm not mad;
Nor horn-mad, see you? Go to, shew yourself
Obedient, and a wife.

CEL:

O heaven!

CORV:

I say it,
Do so.

CEL:

Was this the train?

CORV:

I've told you reasons;
What the physicians have set down; how much
It may concern me; what my engagements are;
My means; and the necessity of those means,
For my recovery: wherefore, if you be
Loyal, and mine, be won, respect my venture.

CEL:

Before your honour?

CORV:

Honour! tut, a breath:
There's no such thing, in nature: a mere term
Invented to awe fools. What is my gold
The worse, for touching, clothes for being look'd on?
Why, this is no more. An old decrepit wretch,
That has no sense, no sinew; takes his meat
With others' fingers; only knows to gape,
When you do scald his gums; a voice; a shadow;

And, what can this man hurt you?
CEL *[ASIDE.]:*
Lord! what spirit
Is this hath enter'd him?
CORV:
And for your fame,
That's such a jig; as if I would go tell it,
Cry it on the Piazza! who shall know it,
But he that cannot speak it, and this fellow,
Whose lips are in my pocket? save yourself,
(If you'll proclaim't, you may,) I know no other,
Shall come to know it.
CEL:
Are heaven and saints then nothing?
Will they be blind or stupid?
CORV:
How!
CEL:
Good sir,
Be jealous still, emulate them; and think
What hate they burn with toward every sin.
CORV:
I grant you: if I thought it were a sin,
I would not urge you. Should I offer this
To some young Frenchman, or hot Tuscan blood
That had read Aretine, conn'd all his prints,
Knew every quirk within lust's labyrinth,
And were professed critic in lechery;
And I would look upon him, and applaud him,
This were a sin: but here, 'tis contrary,
A pious work, mere charity for physic,
And honest polity, to assure mine own.
CEL:
O heaven! canst thou suffer such a change?
VOLP:

Thou art mine honour, Mosca, and my pride,
My joy, my tickling, my delight! Go bring them.
MOS _[ADVANCING.]_:
Please you draw near, sir.
CORV:
Come on, what--
You will not be rebellious? by that light--
MOS:
Sir,
Signior Corvino, here, is come to see you.
VOLP:
Oh!
MOS:
And hearing of the consultation had,
So lately, for your health, is come to offer,
Or rather, sir, to prostitute--
CORV:
Thanks, sweet Mosca.
MOS:
Freely, unask'd, or unintreated--
CORV:
Well.
MOS:
As the true fervent instance of his love,
His own most fair and proper wife; the beauty,
Only of price in Venice--
CORV:
'Tis well urged.
MOS:
To be your comfortress, and to preserve you.
VOLP:
Alas, I am past, already! Pray you, thank him
For his good care and promptness; but for that,
'Tis a vain labour e'en to fight 'gainst heaven;

Applying fire to stone--
[COUGHING.] uh, uh, uh, uh!
Making a dead leaf grow again. I take
His wishes gently, though; and you may tell him,
What I have done for him: marry, my state is hopeless.
Will him to pray for me; and to use his fortune
With reverence, when he comes to't.

MOS:

Do you hear, sir?
Go to him with your wife.

CORV:

Heart of my father!
Wilt thou persist thus? come, I pray thee, come.
Thou seest 'tis nothing, Celia. By this hand,
I shall grow violent. Come, do't, I say.

CEL:

Sir, kill me, rather: I will take down poison,
Eat burning coals, do any thing.--

CORV:

Be damn'd!
Heart, I'll drag thee hence, home, by the hair;
Cry thee a strumpet through the streets; rip up
Thy mouth unto thine ears; and slit thy nose,
Like a raw rotchet!--Do not tempt me; come,
Yield, I am loth--Death! I will buy some slave
Whom I will kill, and bind thee to him, alive;
And at my window hang you forth: devising
Some monstrous crime, which I, in capital letters,
Will eat into thy flesh with aquafortis,
And burning corsives, on this stubborn breast.
Now, by the blood thou hast incensed, I'll do it!

CEL:

Sir, what you please, you may, I am your martyr.

CORV:

Be not thus obstinate, I have not deserved it:

Think who it is intreats you. 'Prithee, sweet;--
Good faith, thou shalt have jewels, gowns, attires,
What thou wilt think, and ask. Do but go kiss him.
Or touch him, but. For my sake.--At my suit.--
This once.--No! not! I shall remember this.
Will you disgrace me thus? Do you thirst my undoing?

MOS:

Nay, gentle lady, be advised.

CORV:

No, no.
She has watch'd her time. Ods precious, this is scurvy,
'Tis very scurvy: and you are--

MOS:

Nay, good, sir.

CORV:

An arrant Locust, by heaven, a locust!
Whore, crocodile, that hast thy tears prepared,
Expecting how thou'lt bid them flow--

MOS:

Nay, 'Pray you, sir!
She will consider.

CEL:

Would my life would serve
To satisfy--

CORV:

S'death! if she would but speak to him,
And save my reputation, it were somewhat;
But spightfully to affect my utter ruin!

MOS:

Ay, now you have put your fortune in her hands.
Why i'faith, it is her modesty, I must quit her.
If you were absent, she would be more coming;
I know it: and dare undertake for her.
What woman can before her husband? 'pray you,

Let us depart, and leave her here.

CORV:

Sweet Celia,
Thou may'st redeem all, yet; I'll say no more:
If not, esteem yourself as lost,--Nay, stay there.

[SHUTS THE DOOR, AND EXIT WITH MOSCA.]

CEL:

O God, and his good angels! whither, whither,
Is shame fled human breasts? that with such ease,
Men dare put off your honours, and their own?
Is that, which ever was a cause of life,
Now placed beneath the basest circumstance,
And modesty an exile made, for money?

VOLP:

Ay, in Corvino, and such earth-fed minds,

[LEAPING FROM HIS COUCH.]

That never tasted the true heaven of love.
Assure thee, Celia, he that would sell thee,
Only for hope of gain, and that uncertain,
He would have sold his part of Paradise
For ready money, had he met a cope-man.
Why art thou mazed to see me thus revived?
Rather applaud thy beauty's miracle;
'Tis thy great work: that hath, not now alone,
But sundry times raised me, in several shapes,
And, but this morning, like a mountebank;
To see thee at thy window: ay, before
I would have left my practice, for thy love,
In varying figures, I would have contended
With the blue Proteus, or the horned flood.
Now art thou welcome.

CEL:

Sir!

VOLP:

Nay, fly me not.
Nor let thy false imagination
That I was bed-rid, make thee think I am so:
Thou shalt not find it. I am, now, as fresh,
As hot, as high, and in as jovial plight,
As when, in that so celebrated scene,
At recitation of our comedy,
For entertainment of the great Valois,
I acted young Antinous; and attracted
The eyes and ears of all the ladies present,
To admire each graceful gesture, note, and footing.

[SINGS.]

Come, my Celia, let us prove,
While we can, the sports of love,
Time will not be ours for ever,
He, at length, our good will sever;
Spend not then his gifts in vain;
Suns, that set, may rise again:
But if once we loose this light,
'Tis with us perpetual night.
Why should we defer our joys?
Fame and rumour are but toys.
Cannot we delude the eyes
Of a few poor household spies?
Or his easier ears beguile,
Thus remooved by our wile?--
'Tis no sin love's fruits to steal:
But the sweet thefts to reveal;
To be taken, to be seen,

These have crimes accounted been.

CEL:

Some serene blast me, or dire lightning strike
This my offending face!

VOLP:

Why droops my Celia?
Thou hast, in place of a base husband, found
A worthy lover: use thy fortune well,
With secrecy and pleasure. See, behold,
What thou art queen of; not in expectation,
As I feed others: but possess'd, and crown'd.
See, here, a rope of pearl; and each, more orient
Than that the brave Egyptian queen caroused:
Dissolve and drink them. See, a carbuncle,
May put out both the eyes of our St Mark;
A diamond, would have bought Lollia Paulina,
When she came in like star-light, hid with jewels,
That were the spoils of provinces; take these,
And wear, and lose them: yet remains an ear-ring
To purchase them again, and this whole state.
A gem but worth a private patrimony,
Is nothing: we will eat such at a meal.
The heads of parrots, tongues of nightingales,
The brains of peacocks, and of estriches,
Shall be our food: and, could we get the phoenix,
Though nature lost her kind, she were our dish.

CEL:

Good sir, these things might move a mind affected
With such delights; but I, whose innocence
Is all I can think wealthy, or worth th' enjoying,
And which, once lost, I have nought to lose beyond it,
Cannot be taken with these sensual baits:
If you have conscience--

VOLP:

'Tis the beggar's virtue,

If thou hast wisdom, hear me, Celia.
Thy baths shall be the juice of July-flowers,
Spirit of roses, and of violets,
The milk of unicorns, and panthers' breath
Gather'd in bags, and mixt with Cretan wines.
Our drink shall be prepared gold and amber;
Which we will take, until my roof whirl round
With the vertigo: and my dwarf shall dance,
My eunuch sing, my fool make up the antic.
Whilst we, in changed shapes, act Ovid's tales,
Thou, like Europa now, and I like Jove,
Then I like Mars, and thou like Erycine:
So, of the rest, till we have quite run through,
And wearied all the fables of the gods.
Then will I have thee in more modern forms,
Attired like some sprightly dame of France,
Brave Tuscan lady, or proud Spanish beauty;
Sometimes, unto the Persian sophy's wife;
Or the grand signior's mistress; and, for change,
To one of our most artful courtezans,
Or some quick Negro, or cold Russian;
And I will meet thee in as many shapes:
Where we may so transfuse our wandering souls,
Out at our lips, and score up sums of pleasures,

[SINGS.]

That the curious shall not know
How to tell them as they flow;
And the envious, when they find
What there number is, be pined.
CEL:
If you have ears that will be pierc'd--or eyes
That can be open'd--a heart that may be touch'd--

Or any part that yet sounds man about you--
If you have touch of holy saints--or heaven--
Do me the grace to let me 'scape--if not,
Be bountiful and kill me. You do know,
I am a creature, hither ill betray'd,
By one, whose shame I would forget it were:
If you will deign me neither of these graces,
Yet feed your wrath, sir, rather than your lust,
(It is a vice comes nearer manliness,)
And punish that unhappy crime of nature,
Which you miscall my beauty; flay my face,
Or poison it with ointments, for seducing
Your blood to this rebellion. Rub these hands,
With what may cause an eating leprosy,
E'en to my bones and marrow: any thing,
That may disfavour me, save in my honour--
And I will kneel to you, pray for you, pay down
A thousand hourly vows, sir, for your health;
Report, and think you virtuous--

VOLP:

Think me cold,
Frosen and impotent, and so report me?
That I had Nestor's hernia, thou wouldst think.
I do degenerate, and abuse my nation,
To play with opportunity thus long;
I should have done the act, and then have parley'd.
Yield, or I'll force thee.

[SEIZES HER.]

CEL:

O! just God!
VOLP:

In vain--
BON *[RUSHING IN]:*

Forbear, foul ravisher, libidinous swine!
Free the forced lady, or thou diest, impostor.
But that I'm loth to snatch thy punishment
Out of the hand of justice, thou shouldst, yet,
Be made the timely sacrifice of vengeance,
Before this altar, and this dross, thy idol.--
Lady, let's quit the place, it is the den
Of villany; fear nought, you have a guard:
And he, ere long, shall meet his just reward.

[EXEUNT BON. AND CEL.]

VOLP:
Fall on me, roof, and bury me in ruin!
Become my grave, that wert my shelter! O!
I am unmask'd, unspirited, undone,
Betray'd to beggary, to infamy--

[ENTER MOSCA, WOUNDED AND BLEEDING.]

MOS:
Where shall I run, most wretched shame of men,
To beat out my unlucky brains?
VOLP:
Here, here.
What! dost thou bleed?
MOS:
O that his well-driv'n sword
Had been so courteous to have cleft me down
Unto the navel; ere I lived to see
My life, my hopes, my spirits, my patron, all
Thus desperately engaged, by my error!
VOLP:
Woe on thy fortune!

MOS:

And my follies, sir.

VOLP:

Thou hast made me miserable.

MOS:

And myself, sir.
Who would have thought he would have harken'd, so?

VOLP:

What shall we do?

MOS:

I know not; if my heart
Could expiate the mischance, I'd pluck it out.
Will you be pleased to hang me? or cut my throat?
And I'll requite you, sir. Let us die like Romans,
Since we have lived like Grecians.

[KNOCKING WITHIN.]

VOLP:

Hark! who's there?
I hear some footing; officers, the saffi,
Come to apprehend us! I do feel the brand
Hissing already at my forehead; now,
Mine ears are boring.

MOS:

To your couch, sir, you,
Make that place good, however.

[VOLPONE LIES DOWN, AS BEFORE.]

--Guilty men
Suspect what they deserve still.

[ENTER CORBACCIO.]

Signior Corbaccio!
CORB:

Why, how now, Mosca?
MOS:

O, undone, amazed, sir.
Your son, I know not by what accident,
Acquainted with your purpose to my patron,
Touching your Will, and making him your heir,
Enter'd our house with violence, his sword drawn
Sought for you, call'd you wretch, unnatural,
Vow'd he would kill you.
CORB:

Me!
MOS:

Yes, and my patron.
CORB:

This act shall disinherit him indeed;
Here is the Will.
MOS:

'Tis well, sir.
CORB:

Right and well:
Be you as careful now for me.

[ENTER VOLTORE, BEHIND.]

MOS:

My life, sir,
Is not more tender'd; I am only yours.
CORB:

How does he? will he die shortly, think'st thou?
MOS:

I fear
He'll outlast May.

CORB:

To-day?

MOS:

No, last out May, sir.

CORB:

Could'st thou not give him a dram?

MOS:

O, by no means, sir.

CORB:

Nay, I'll not bid you.

VOLT *[COMING FORWARD.]:*

This is a knave, I see.

MOS *[SEEING VOLTORE.]:*

How! signior Voltore!

[ASIDE.] did he hear me?

VOLT:

Parasite!

MOS:

Who's that?--O, sir, most timely welcome--

VOLT:

Scarce,

To the discovery of your tricks, I fear.

You are his, ONLY? and mine, also? are you not?

MOS:

Who? I, sir?

VOLT:

You, sir. What device is this

About a Will?

MOS:

A plot for you, sir.

VOLT:

Come,

Put not your foists upon me; I shall scent them.

MOS:

Did you not hear it?

VOLT:

Yes, I hear Corbaccio

Hath made your patron there his heir.

MOS:

'Tis true,

By my device, drawn to it by my plot,

With hope--

VOLT:

Your patron should reciprocate?

And you have promised?

MOS:

For your good, I did, sir.

Nay, more, I told his son, brought, hid him here,

Where he might hear his father pass the deed:

Being persuaded to it by this thought, sir,

That the unnaturalness, first, of the act,

And then his father's oft disclaiming in him,

(Which I did mean t'help on,) would sure enrage him

To do some violence upon his parent,

On which the law should take sufficient hold,

And you be stated in a double hope:

Truth be my comfort, and my conscience,

My only aim was to dig you a fortune

Out of these two old rotten sepulchres--

VOLT:

I cry thee mercy, Mosca.

MOS:

Worth your patience,

And your great merit, sir. And see the change!

VOLT:

Why, what success?

MOS:

Most happless! you must help, sir.

Whilst we expected the old raven, in comes

Corvino's wife, sent hither by her husband--
VOLT:

What, with a present?
MOS:

No, sir, on visitation;
(I'll tell you how anon;) and staying long,
The youth he grows impatient, rushes forth,
Seizeth the lady, wounds me, makes her swear
(Or he would murder her, that was his vow)
To affirm my patron to have done her rape:
Which how unlike it is, you see! and hence,
With that pretext he's gone, to accuse his father,
Defame my patron, defeat you--
VOLT:

Where is her husband?
Let him be sent for straight.
MOS:

Sir, I'll go fetch him.
VOLT:

Bring him to the Scrutineo.
MOS:

Sir, I will.
VOLT:

This must be stopt.
MOS:

O you do nobly, sir.
Alas, 'twas labor'd all, sir, for your good;
Nor was there want of counsel in the plot:
But fortune can, at any time, o'erthrow
The projects of a hundred learned clerks, sir.
CORB *[LISTENING]:*

What's that?
VOLT:

Will't please you, sir, to go along?

[EXIT CORBACCIO, FOLLOWED BY VOLTORE.]

MOS:
Patron, go in, and pray for our success.
VOLP *[RISING FROM HIS COUCH.]:*
Need makes devotion:
heaven your labour bless!

[EXEUNT.]

ACT 4.

SCENE 4.1.

A STREET.

[ENTER SIR POLITICK WOULD-BE AND PEREGRINE.]

SIR P:
> I told you, sir, it was a plot: you see
> What observation is! You mention'd me,
> For some instructions: I will tell you, sir,
> (Since we are met here in this height of Venice,)
> Some few perticulars I have set down,
> Only for this meridian, fit to be known
> Of your crude traveller, and they are these.
> I will not touch, sir, at your phrase, or clothes,
> For they are old.

PER:
> Sir, I have better.

SIR P:
> Pardon,
> I meant, as they are themes.

PER:
> O, sir, proceed:
> I'll slander you no more of wit, good sir.

SIR P:
> First, for your garb, it must be grave and serious,
> Very reserv'd, and lock'd; not tell a secret
> On any terms, not to your father; scarce
> A fable, but with caution; make sure choice

Both of your company, and discourse; beware
You never speak a truth--
PER:
How!
SIR P:
Not to strangers,
For those be they you must converse with, most;
Others I would not know, sir, but at distance,
So as I still might be a saver in them:
You shall have tricks else past upon you hourly.
And then, for your religion, profess none,
But wonder at the diversity, of all:
And, for your part, protest, were there no other
But simply the laws o' the land, you could content you,
Nic. Machiavel, and Monsieur Bodin, both
Were of this mind. Then must you learn the use
And handling of your silver fork at meals;
The metal of your glass; (these are main matters
With your Italian;) and to know the hour
When you must eat your melons, and your figs.
PER:
Is that a point of state too?
SIR P:
Here it is,
For your Venetian, if he see a man
Preposterous in the least, he has him straight;
He has; he strips him. I'll acquaint you, sir,
I now have lived here, 'tis some fourteen months
Within the first week of my landing here,
All took me for a citizen of Venice:
I knew the forms, so well--
PER *[ASIDE.]:*
And nothing else.
SIR P:

I had read Contarene, took me a house,
Dealt with my Jews to furnish it with moveables--
Well, if I could but find one man, one man
To mine own heart, whom I durst trust, I would--

PER:

What, what, sir?

SIR P:

Make him rich; make him a fortune:
He should not think again. I would command it.

PER:

As how?

SIR P:

With certain projects that I have;
Which I may not discover.

PER *[ASIDE.]:*

If I had
But one to wager with, I would lay odds now,
He tells me instantly.

SIR P:

One is, and that
I care not greatly who knows, to serve the state
Of Venice with red herrings for three years,
And at a certain rate, from Rotterdam,
Where I have correspondence. There's a letter,
Sent me from one of the states, and to that purpose:
He cannot write his name, but that's his mark.

PER:

He's a chandler?

SIR P:

No, a cheesemonger.
There are some others too with whom I treat
About the same negociation;
And I will undertake it: for, 'tis thus.
I'll do't with ease, I have cast it all: Your hoy
Carries but three men in her, and a boy;

And she shall make me three returns a year:
So, if there come but one of three, I save,
If two, I can defalk:--but this is now,
If my main project fail.

PER:

Then you have others?

SIR P:

I should be loth to draw the subtle air
Of such a place, without my thousand aims.
I'll not dissemble, sir: where'er I come,
I love to be considerative; and 'tis true,
I have at my free hours thought upon
Some certain goods unto the state of Venice,
Which I do call "my Cautions;" and, sir, which
I mean, in hope of pension, to propound
To the Great Council, then unto the Forty,
So to the Ten. My means are made already--

PER:

By whom?

SIR P:

Sir, one that, though his place be obscure,
Yet he can sway, and they will hear him. He's
A commandador.

PER:

What! a common serjeant?

SIR P:

Sir, such as they are, put it in their mouths,
What they should say, sometimes; as well as greater:
I think I have my notes to shew you--

[SEARCHING HIS POCKETS.]

PER:

Good sir.

SIR P:

But you shall swear unto me, on your gentry,
Not to anticipate--

PER:

I, sir!

SIR P:

Nor reveal
A circumstance--My paper is not with me.

PER:

O, but you can remember, sir.

SIR P:

My first is
Concerning tinder-boxes. You must know,
No family is here, without its box.
Now, sir, it being so portable a thing,
Put case, that you or I were ill affected
Unto the state, sir; with it in our pockets,
Might not I go into the Arsenal,
Or you, come out again, and none the wiser?

PER:

Except yourself, sir.

SIR P:

Go to, then. I therefore
Advertise to the state, how fit it were,
That none but such as were known patriots,
Sound lovers of their country, should be suffer'd
To enjoy them in their houses; and even those
Seal'd at some office, and at such a bigness
As might not lurk in pockets.

PER:

Admirable!

SIR P:

My next is, how to enquire, and be resolv'd,
By present demonstration, whether a ship,
Newly arrived from Soria, or from

Any suspected part of all the Levant,
Be guilty of the plague: and where they use
To lie out forty, fifty days, sometimes,
About the Lazaretto, for their trial;
I'll save that charge and loss unto the merchant,
And in an hour clear the doubt.

PER:

Indeed, sir!

SIR P:

Or--I will lose my labour.

PER:

'My faith, that's much.

SIR P:

Nay, sir, conceive me. It will cost me in onions,
Some thirty livres--

PER:

Which is one pound sterling.

SIR P:

Beside my water-works: for this I do, sir.
First, I bring in your ship 'twixt two brick walls;
But those the state shall venture: On the one
I strain me a fair tarpauling, and in that
I stick my onions, cut in halves: the other
Is full of loop-holes, out at which I thrust
The noses of my bellows; and those bellows
I keep, with water-works, in perpetual motion,
Which is the easiest matter of a hundred.
Now, sir, your onion, which doth naturally
Attract the infection, and your bellows blowing
The air upon him, will show, instantly,
By his changed colour, if there be contagion;
Or else remain as fair as at the first.
--Now it is known, 'tis nothing.

PER:

You are right, sir.

SIR P:

I would I had my note.

PER:

'Faith, so would I:
But you have done well for once, sir.

SIR P:

Were I false,
Or would be made so, I could shew you reasons
How I could sell this state now, to the Turk;
Spite of their galleys, or their--

[EXAMINING HIS PAPERS.]

PER:

Pray you, sir Pol.

SIR P:

I have them not about me.

PER:

That I fear'd.
They are there, sir.

SIR P:

No. This is my diary,
Wherein I note my actions of the day.

PER:

Pray you let's see, sir. What is here?

[READS.]

"Notandum,
A rat had gnawn my spur-leathers; notwithstanding,
I put on new, and did go forth: but first
I threw three beans over the threshold. Item,
I went and bought two tooth-picks, whereof one
I burst immediatly, in a discourse

With a Dutch merchant, 'bout ragion del stato.
From him I went and paid a moccinigo,
For piecing my silk stockings; by the way
I cheapen'd sprats; and at St. Mark's I urined."
'Faith, these are politic notes!

SIR P:

Sir, I do slip
No action of my life, but thus I quote it.

PER:

Believe me, it is wise!

SIR P:

Nay, sir, read forth.

[ENTER, AT A DISTANCE, LADY POLITICK-WOULD BE, NANO, AND TWO WAITING-WOMEN.]

LADY P:

Where should this loose knight be, trow?
sure he's housed.

NAN:

Why, then he's fast.

LADY P:

Ay, he plays both with me.
I pray you, stay. This heat will do more harm
To my complexion, than his heart is worth;
(I do not care to hinder, but to take him.)

[RUBBING HER CHEEKS.]

How it comes off!

1 WOM:

My master's yonder.

LADY P:

Where?

1 WOM:

With a young gentleman.

LADY P:

That same's the party;
In man's apparel! 'Pray you, sir, jog my knight:
I'll be tender to his reputation,
However he demerit.

SIR P *[SEEING HER]:*

My lady!

PER:

Where?

SIR P:

'Tis she indeed, sir; you shall know her. She is,
Were she not mine, a lady of that merit,
For fashion and behaviour; and, for beauty
I durst compare--

PER:

It seems you are not jealous,
That dare commend her.

SIR P:

Nay, and for discourse--

PER:

Being your wife, she cannot miss that.

SIR P *[INTRODUCING PER.]:*

Madam,
Here is a gentleman, pray you, use him fairly;
He seems a youth, but he is--

LADY P:

None.

SIR P:

Yes, one
Has put his face as soon into the world--

LADY P:

You mean, as early? but to-day?

SIR P:

How's this?
LADY P:
Why, in this habit, sir; you apprehend me:--
Well, master Would-be, this doth not become you;
I had thought the odour, sir, of your good name,
Had been more precious to you; that you would not
Have done this dire massacre on your honour;
One of your gravity and rank besides!
But knights, I see, care little for the oath
They make to ladies; chiefly, their own ladies.
SIR P:
Now by my spurs, the symbol of my knighthood,--
PER *[ASIDE.]:*
Lord, how his brain is humbled for an oath!
SIR P:
I reach you not.
LADY P:
Right, sir, your policy
May bear it through, thus.

[TO PER.]

sir, a word with you.
I would be loth to contest publicly
With any gentlewoman, or to seem
Froward, or violent, as the courtier says;
It comes too near rusticity in a lady,
Which I would shun by all means: and however
I may deserve from master Would-be, yet
T'have one fair gentlewoman thus be made
The unkind instrument to wrong another,
And one she knows not, ay, and to persever;
In my poor judgment, is not warranted
From being a solecism in our sex,

If not in manners.
PER:
How is this!
SIR P:
Sweet madam,
Come nearer to your aim.
LADY P:
Marry, and will, sir.
Since you provoke me with your impudence,
And laughter of your light land-syren here,
Your Sporus, your hermaphrodite--
PER:
What's here?
Poetic fury, and historic storms?
SIR P:
The gentleman, believe it, is of worth,
And of our nation.
LADY P:
Ay, your White-friars nation.
Come, I blush for you, master Would-be, I;
And am asham'd you should have no more forehead,
Than thus to be the patron, or St. George,
To a lewd harlot, a base fricatrice,
A female devil, in a male outside.
SIR P:
Nay,
And you be such a one, I must bid adieu
To your delights. The case appears too liquid.

[EXIT.]

LADY P:
Ay, you may carry't clear, with your state-face!--
But for your carnival concupiscence,
Who here is fled for liberty of conscience,

From furious persecution of the marshal,
Her will I dis'ple.
PER:
This is fine, i'faith!
And do you use this often? Is this part
Of your wit's exercise, 'gainst you have occasion?
Madam--
LADY P:
Go to, sir.
PER:
Do you hear me, lady?
Why, if your knight have set you to beg shirts,
Or to invite me home, you might have done it
A nearer way, by far:
LADY P:
This cannot work you
Out of my snare.
PER:
Why, am I in it, then?
Indeed your husband told me you were fair,
And so you are; only your nose inclines,
That side that's next the sun, to the queen-apple.
LADY P:
This cannot be endur'd by any patience.

[ENTER MOSCA.]

MOS:
What is the matter, madam?
LADY P:
If the Senate
Right not my quest in this; I'll protest them
To all the world, no aristocracy.
MOS:

What is the injury, lady?

LADY P:

Why, the callet
You told me of, here I have ta'en disguised.

MOS:

Who? this! what means your ladyship? the creature
I mention'd to you is apprehended now,
Before the senate; you shall see her--

LADY P:

Where?

MOS:

I'll bring you to her. This young gentleman,
I saw him land this morning at the port.

LADY P:

Is't possible! how has my judgment wander'd?
Sir, I must, blushing, say to you, I have err'd;
And plead your pardon.

PER:

What, more changes yet!

LADY P:

I hope you have not the malice to remember
A gentlewoman's passion. If you stay
In Venice here, please you to use me, sir--

MOS:

Will you go, madam?

LADY P:

'Pray you, sir, use me. In faith,
The more you see me, the more I shall conceive
You have forgot our quarrel.

*[EXEUNT LADY WOULD-BE, MOSCA, NANO, AND WAITING-
WOMEN.]*

PER:

This is rare!

Sir Politick Would-be? no; sir Politick Bawd.
To bring me thus acquainted with his wife!
Well, wise sir Pol, since you have practised thus
Upon my freshman-ship, I'll try your salt-head,
What proof it is against a counter-plot.

[EXIT.]

SCENE 4.2.

THE SCRUTINEO, OR SENATE-HOUSE.

ENTER VOLTORE, CORBACCIO, CORVINO, AND MOSCA.

VOLT:
Well, now you know the carriage of the business,
Your constancy is all that is required
Unto the safety of it.

MOS:
Is the lie
Safely convey'd amongst us? is that sure?
Knows every man his burden?

CORV:
Yes.

MOS:
Then shrink not.

CORV:
But knows the advocate the truth?

MOS:
O, sir,
By no means; I devised a formal tale,
That salv'd your reputation. But be valiant, sir.

CORV:
I fear no one but him, that this his pleading

Should make him stand for a co-heir--
MOS:
Co-halter!
Hang him; we will but use his tongue, his noise,
As we do croakers here.
CORV:
Ay, what shall he do?
MOS:
When we have done, you mean?
CORV:
Yes.
MOS:
Why, we'll think:
Sell him for mummia; he's half dust already.

[TO VOLTORE.]

Do not you smile, to see this buffalo,
How he does sport it with his head?

[ASIDE.]

--I should,
If all were well and past.

[TO CORBACCIO.]

--Sir, only you
Are he that shall enjoy the crop of all,
And these not know for whom they toil.
CORB:
Ay, peace.
MOS
[TURNING TO CORVINO.]:
But you shall eat it.

Much! *[ASIDE.]*

[TO VOLTORE.]

    --Worshipful sir,
Mercury sit upon your thundering tongue,
Or the French Hercules, and make your language
As conquering as his club, to beat along,
As with a tempest, flat, our adversaries;
But much more yours, sir.

VOLT:
Here they come, have done.

MOS:
I have another witness, if you need, sir,
I can produce.

VOLT:
Who is it?

MOS:
Sir, I have her.

[ENTER AVOCATORI AND TAKE THEIR SEATS, BONARIO, CELIA, NOTARIO, COMMANDADORI, SAFFI, AND OTHER OFFICERS OF JUSTICE.]

1 AVOC:
The like of this the senate never heard of.

2 AVOC:
'Twill come most strange to them when we report it.

4 AVOC:
The gentlewoman has been ever held
Of unreproved name.

3 AVOC:
So has the youth.

4 AVOC:

The more unnatural part that of his father.

2 AVOC:

More of the husband.

1 AVOC:

I not know to give
His act a name, it is so monstrous!

4 AVOC:

But the impostor, he's a thing created
To exceed example!

1 AVOC:

And all after-times!

2 AVOC:

I never heard a true voluptuary
Discribed, but him.

3 AVOC:

Appear yet those were cited?

NOT:

All, but the old magnifico, Volpone.

1 AVOC:

Why is not he here?

MOS:

Please your fatherhoods,
Here is his advocate: himself's so weak,
So feeble--

4 AVOC:

What are you?

BON:

His parasite,
His knave, his pandar--I beseech the court,
He may be forced to come, that your grave eyes
May bear strong witness of his strange impostures.

VOLT:

Upon my faith and credit with your virtues,
He is not able to endure the air.

2 AVOC:

Bring him, however.
3 AVOC:
We will see him.
4 AVOC:
Fetch him.
VOLT:
Your fatherhoods fit pleasures be obey'd;

[EXEUNT OFFICERS.]

But sure, the sight will rather move your pities,
Than indignation. May it please the court,
In the mean time, he may be heard in me;
I know this place most void of prejudice,
And therefore crave it, since we have no reason
To fear our truth should hurt our cause.
3 AVOC:
Speak free.
VOLT:
Then know, most honour'd fathers, I must now
Discover to your strangely abused ears,
The most prodigious and most frontless piece
Of solid impudence, and treachery,
That ever vicious nature yet brought forth
To shame the state of Venice. This lewd woman,
That wants no artificial looks or tears
To help the vizor she has now put on,
Hath long been known a close adulteress,
To that lascivious youth there; not suspected,
I say, but known, and taken in the act
With him; and by this man, the easy husband,
Pardon'd: whose timeless bounty makes him now
Stand here, the most unhappy, innocent person,
That ever man's own goodness made accused.

For these not knowing how to owe a gift
Of that dear grace, but with their shame; being placed
So above all powers of their gratitude,
Began to hate the benefit; and, in place
Of thanks, devise to extirpe the memory
Of such an act: wherein I pray your fatherhoods
To observe the malice, yea, the rage of creatures
Discover'd in their evils; and what heart
Such take, even from their crimes:--but that anon
Will more appear.--This gentleman, the father,
Hearing of this foul fact, with many others,
Which daily struck at his too tender ears,
And grieved in nothing more than that he could not
Preserve himself a parent, (his son's ills
Growing to that strange flood,) at last decreed
To disinherit him.

1 AVOC:

These be strange turns!

2 AVOC:

The young man's fame was ever fair and honest.

VOLT:

So much more full of danger is his vice,
That can beguile so under shade of virtue.
But, as I said, my honour'd sires, his father
Having this settled purpose, by what means
To him betray'd, we know not, and this day
Appointed for the deed; that parricide,
I cannot style him better, by confederacy
Preparing this his paramour to be there,
Enter'd Volpone's house, (who was the man,
Your fatherhoods must understand, design'd
For the inheritance,) there sought his father:--
But with what purpose sought he him, my lords?
I tremble to pronounce it, that a son
Unto a father, and to such a father,

Should have so foul, felonious intent!
It was to murder him: when being prevented
By his more happy absence, what then did he?
Not check his wicked thoughts; no, now new deeds,
(Mischief doth ever end where it begins)
An act of horror, fathers! he dragg'd forth
The aged gentleman that had there lain bed-rid
Three years and more, out of his innocent couch,
Naked upon the floor, there left him; wounded
His servant in the face: and, with this strumpet
The stale to his forged practice, who was glad
To be so active,--(I shall here desire
Your fatherhoods to note but my collections,
As most remarkable,--) thought at once to stop
His father's ends; discredit his free choice
In the old gentleman, redeem themselves,
By laying infamy upon this man,
To whom, with blushing, they should owe their lives.

1 AVOC:

What proofs have you of this?

BON:

Most honoured fathers,
I humbly crave there be no credit given
To this man's mercenary tongue.

2 AVOC:

Forbear.

BON:

His soul moves in his fee.

3 AVOC:

O, sir.

BON:

This fellow,
For six sols more, would plead against his Maker.

1 AVOC:

You do forget yourself.

VOLT:

Nay, nay, grave fathers,
Let him have scope: can any man imagine
That he will spare his accuser, that would not
Have spared his parent?

1 AVOC:

Well, produce your proofs.

CEL:

I would I could forget I were a creature.

VOLT:

Signior Corbaccio.

[CORBACCIO COMES FORWARD.]

1 AVOC:

What is he?

VOLT:

The father.

2 AVOC:

Has he had an oath?

NOT:

Yes.

CORB:

What must I do now?

NOT:

Your testimony's craved.

CORB:

Speak to the knave?
I'll have my mouth first stopt with earth; my heart
Abhors his knowledge: I disclaim in him.

1 AVOC:

But for what cause?

CORB:

The mere portent of nature!

He is an utter stranger to my loins.
BON:
Have they made you to this?
CORB:
I will not hear thee,
Monster of men, swine, goat, wolf, parricide!
Speak not, thou viper.
BON:
Sir, I will sit down,
And rather wish my innocence should suffer,
Then I resist the authority of a father.
VOLT:
Signior Corvino!

[CORVINO COMES FORWARD.]

2 AVOC:
This is strange.
1 AVOC:
Who's this?
NOT:
The husband.
4 AVOC:
Is he sworn?
NOT:
He is.
3 AVOC:
Speak, then.
CORV:
This woman, please your fatherhoods, is a whore,
Of most hot exercise, more than a partrich,
Upon record--
1 AVOC:
No more.

CORV:

Neighs like a jennet.

NOT:

Preserve the honour of the court.

CORV:

I shall,
And modesty of your most reverend ears.
And yet I hope that I may say, these eyes
Have seen her glued unto that piece of cedar,
That fine well-timber'd gallant; and that here
The letters may be read, through the horn,
That make the story perfect.

MOS:

Excellent! sir.

CORV

[ASIDE TO MOSCA.]:
There's no shame in this now, is there?

MOS:

None.

CORV:

Or if I said, I hoped that she were onward
To her damnation, if there be a hell
Greater than whore and woman; a good catholic
May make the doubt.

3 AVOC:

His grief hath made him frantic.

1 AVOC:

Remove him hence.

2 AVOC:

Look to the woman.

[CELIA SWOONS.]

CORV:

Rare!

Prettily feign'd, again!

4 AVOC:

Stand from about her.

1 AVOC:

Give her the air.

3 AVOC *[TO MOSCA.]:*

What can you say?

MOS:

My wound,
May it please your wisdoms, speaks for me, received
In aid of my good patron, when he mist
His sought-for father, when that well-taught dame
Had her cue given her, to cry out, A rape!

BON:

O most laid impudence! Fathers--

3 AVOC:

Sir, be silent;
You had your hearing free, so must they theirs.

2 AVOC:

I do begin to doubt the imposture here.

4 AVOC:

This woman has too many moods.

VOLT:

Grave fathers,
She is a creature of a most profest
And prostituted lewdness.

CORV:

Most impetuous,
Unsatisfied, grave fathers!

VOLT:

May her feignings
Not take your wisdoms: but this day she baited
A stranger, a grave knight, with her loose eyes,
And more lascivious kisses. This man saw them

Together on the water in a gondola.
MOS:
Here is the lady herself, that saw them too;
Without; who then had in the open streets
Pursued them, but for saving her knight's honour.
1 AVOC:
Produce that lady.
2 AVOC:
Let her come.

[EXIT MOSCA.]

4 AVOC:
These things,
They strike with wonder!
3 AVOC:
I am turn'd a stone.

[RE-ENTER MOSCA WITH LADY WOULD-BE.]

MOS:
Be resolute, madam.
LADY P:
Ay, this same is she.

[POINTING TO CELIA.]

Out, thou chameleon harlot! now thine eyes
Vie tears with the hyaena. Dar'st thou look
Upon my wronged face?--I cry your pardons,
I fear I have forgettingly transgrest
Against the dignity of the court--
2 AVOC:
No, madam.
LADY P:

And been exorbitant--
2 AVOC:
You have not, lady.
4 AVOC:
These proofs are strong.
LADY P:
Surely, I had no purpose
To scandalise your honours, or my sex's.
3 AVOC:
We do believe it.
LADY P:
Surely, you may believe it.
2 AVOC:
Madam, we do.
LADY P:
Indeed, you may; my breeding
Is not so coarse--
1 AVOC:
We know it.
LADY P:
To offend
With pertinacy--
3 AVOC:
Lady--
LADY P:
Such a presence!
No surely.
1 AVOC:
We well think it.
LADY P:
You may think it.
1 AVOC:
Let her o'ercome. What witnesses have you
To make good your report?

BON:

Our consciences.

CEL:

And heaven, that never fails the innocent.

4 AVOC:

These are no testimonies.

BON:

Not in your courts,

Where multitude, and clamour overcomes.

1 AVOC:

Nay, then you do wax insolent.

[RE-ENTER OFFICERS, BEARING VOLPONE ON A COUCH.]

VOLT:

Here, here,

The testimony comes, that will convince,

And put to utter dumbness their bold tongues:

See here, grave fathers, here's the ravisher,

The rider on men's wives, the great impostor,

The grand voluptuary! Do you not think

These limbs should affect venery? or these eyes

Covet a concubine? pray you mark these hands;

Are they not fit to stroke a lady's breasts?--

Perhaps he doth dissemble!

BON:

So he does.

VOLT:

Would you have him tortured?

BON:

I would have him proved.

VOLT:

Best try him then with goads, or burning irons;

Put him to the strappado: I have heard

The rack hath cured the gout; 'faith, give it him,

And help him of a malady; be courteous.
I'll undertake, before these honour'd fathers,
He shall have yet as many left diseases,
As she has known adulterers, or thou strumpets.--
O, my most equal hearers, if these deeds,
Acts of this bold and most exorbitant strain,
May pass with sufferance; what one citizen
But owes the forfeit of his life, yea, fame,
To him that dares traduce him? which of you
Are safe, my honour'd fathers? I would ask,
With leave of your grave fatherhoods, if their plot
Have any face or colour like to truth?
Or if, unto the dullest nostril here,
It smell not rank, and most abhorred slander?
I crave your care of this good gentleman,
Whose life is much endanger'd by their fable;
And as for them, I will conclude with this,
That vicious persons, when they're hot and flesh'd
In impious acts, their constancy abounds:
Damn'd deeds are done with greatest confidence.

1 AVOC:

Take them to custody, and sever them.

2 AVOC:

'Tis pity two such prodigies should live.

1 AVOC:

Let the old gentleman be return'd with care;

[EXEUNT OFFICERS WITH VOLPONE.]

I'm sorry our credulity hath wrong'd him.

4 AVOC:

These are two creatures!

3 AVOC:

I've an earthquake in me.

2 AVOC:
>Their shame, even in their cradles, fled their faces.

4 AVOC *[TO VOLT.]*:
>You have done a worthy service to the state, sir,
>In their discovery.

1 AVOC:
>You shall hear, ere night,
>What punishment the court decrees upon them.

[EXEUNT AVOCAT., NOT., AND OFFICERS WITH BONARIO AND CELIA.]

VOLT:
>We thank your fatherhoods.--How like you it?

MOS:
>Rare.
>I'd have your tongue, sir, tipt with gold for this;
>I'd have you be the heir to the whole city;
>The earth I'd have want men, ere you want living:
>They're bound to erect your statue in St. Mark's.
>Signior Corvino, I would have you go
>And shew yourself, that you have conquer'd.

CORV:
>Yes.

MOS:
>It was much better that you should profess
>Yourself a cuckold thus, than that the other
>Should have been prov'd.

CORV:
>Nay, I consider'd that:
>Now it is her fault:

MOS:
>Then it had been yours.

CORV:
>True; I do doubt this advocate still.

MOS:

I'faith,
You need not, I dare ease you of that care.

CORV:

I trust thee, Mosca.

[EXIT.]

MOS:

As your own soul, sir.

CORB:

Mosca!

MOS:

Now for your business, sir.

CORB:

How! have you business?

MOS:

Yes, your's, sir.

CORB:

O, none else?

MOS:

None else, not I.

CORB:

Be careful, then.

MOS:

Rest you with both your eyes, sir.

CORB:

Dispatch it.

MOS:

Instantly.

CORB:

And look that all,
Whatever, be put in, jewels, plate, moneys,
Household stuff, bedding, curtains.

MOS:

Curtain-rings, sir.
Only the advocate's fee must be deducted.

CORB:

I'll pay him now; you'll be too prodigal.

MOS:

Sir, I must tender it.

CORB:

Two chequines is well?

MOS:

No, six, sir.

CORB:

'Tis too much.

MOS:

He talk'd a great while;
You must consider that, sir.

CORB:

Well, there's three--

MOS:

I'll give it him.

CORB:

Do so, and there's for thee.

[EXIT.]

MOS [ASIDE.]:

Bountiful bones! What horrid strange offence
Did he commit 'gainst nature, in his youth,
Worthy this age?
[TO VOLT.]--You see, sir, how I work
Unto your ends; take you no notice.

VOLT:

No,
I'll leave you.

[EXIT.]

MOS:

All is yours, the devil and all:
Good advocate!--Madam, I'll bring you home.

LADY P:

No, I'll go see your patron.

MOS:

That you shall not:
I'll tell you why. My purpose is to urge
My patron to reform his Will; and for
The zeal you have shewn to-day, whereas before
You were but third or fourth, you shall be now
Put in the first; which would appear as begg'd,
If you were present. Therefore--

LADY P:

You shall sway me.

[EXEUNT.]

ACT 5.

SCENE 5.1

A ROOM IN VOLPONE'S HOUSE.

ENTER VOLPONE.

VOLP:
Well, I am here, and all this brunt is past.
I ne'er was in dislike with my disguise
Till this fled moment; here 'twas good, in private;
But in your public,--cave whilst I breathe.
'Fore God, my left leg began to have the cramp,
And I apprehended straight some power had struck me
With a dead palsy: Well! I must be merry,
And shake it off. A many of these fears
Would put me into some villanous disease,
Should they come thick upon me: I'll prevent 'em.
Give me a bowl of lusty wine, to fright
This humour from my heart.

[DRINKS.]

Hum, hum, hum!
'Tis almost gone already; I shall conquer.
Any device, now, of rare ingenious knavery,
That would possess me with a violent laughter,
Would make me up again.

[DINKS AGAIN.]

So, so, so, so!
This heat is life; 'tis blood by this time:--Mosca!

[ENTER MOSCA.]

MOS:
How now, sir? does the day look clear again?
Are we recover'd, and wrought out of error,
Into our way, to see our path before us?
Is our trade free once more?
VOLP:
Exquisite Mosca!
MOS:
Was it not carried learnedly?
VOLP:
And stoutly:
Good wits are greatest in extremities.
MOS:
It were a folly beyond thought, to trust
Any grand act unto a cowardly spirit:
You are not taken with it enough, methinks?
VOLP:
O, more than if I had enjoy'd the wench:
The pleasure of all woman-kind's not like it.
MOS:
Why now you speak, sir. We must here be fix'd;
Here we must rest; this is our master-peice;
We cannot think to go beyond this.
VOLP:
True.
Thou hast play'd thy prize, my precious Mosca.
MOS:
Nay, sir,

To gull the court--

VOLP:

And quite divert the torrent
Upon the innocent.

MOS:

Yes, and to make
So rare a music out of discords--

VOLP:

Right.
That yet to me's the strangest, how thou hast borne it!
That these, being so divided 'mongst themselves,
Should not scent somewhat, or in me or thee,
Or doubt their own side.

MOS:

True, they will not see't.
Too much light blinds them, I think. Each of them
Is so possest and stuft with his own hopes,
That any thing unto the contrary,
Never so true, or never so apparent,
Never so palpable, they will resist it--

VOLP:

Like a temptation of the devil.

MOS:

Right, sir.
Merchants may talk of trade, and your great signiors
Of land that yields well; but if Italy
Have any glebe more fruitful than these fellows,
I am deceiv'd. Did not your advocate rare?

VOLP:

O--"My most honour'd fathers, my grave fathers,
Under correction of your fatherhoods,
What face of truth is here? If these strange deeds
May pass, most honour'd fathers"--I had much ado
To forbear laughing.

MOS:

It seem'd to me, you sweat, sir.

VOLP:

In troth, I did a little.

MOS:

But confess, sir,
Were you not daunted?

VOLP:

In good faith, I was
A little in a mist, but not dejected;
Never, but still my self.

MOS:

I think it, sir.
Now, so truth help me, I must needs say this, sir,
And out of conscience for your advocate:
He has taken pains, in faith, sir, and deserv'd,
In my poor judgment, I speak it under favour,
Not to contrary you, sir, very richly--
Well--to be cozen'd.

VOLP:

Troth, and I think so too,
By that I heard him, in the latter end.

MOS:

O, but before, sir: had you heard him first
Draw it to certain heads, then aggravate,
Then use his vehement figures--I look'd still
When he would shift a shirt: and, doing this
Out of pure love, no hope of gain--

VOLP:

'Tis right.
I cannot answer him, Mosca, as I would,
Not yet; but for thy sake, at thy entreaty,
I will begin, even now--to vex them all,
This very instant.

MOS:

Good sir.
VOLP:
Call the dwarf
And eunuch forth.
MOS:
Castrone, Nano!

[ENTER CASTRONE AND NANO.]

NANO:
Here.
VOLP:
Shall we have a jig now?
MOS:
What you please, sir.
VOLP:
Go,
Straight give out about the streets, you two,
That I am dead; do it with constancy,
Sadly, do you hear? impute it to the grief
Of this late slander.

[EXEUNT CAST. AND NANO.]

MOS:
What do you mean, sir?
VOLP:
O,
I shall have instantly my Vulture, Crow,
Raven, come flying hither, on the news,
To peck for carrion, my she-wolfe, and all,
Greedy, and full of expectation--
MOS:
And then to have it ravish'd from their mouths!
VOLP:

'Tis true. I will have thee put on a gown,
And take upon thee, as thou wert mine heir:
Shew them a will; Open that chest, and reach
Forth one of those that has the blanks; I'll straight
Put in thy name.

MOS *[GIVES HIM A PAPER.]:*

It will be rare, sir.

VOLP:

Ay,
When they ev'n gape, and find themselves deluded--

MOS:

Yes.

VOLP:

And thou use them scurvily!
Dispatch, get on thy gown.

MOS *[PUTTING ON A GOWN.]:*

But, what, sir, if they ask
After the body?

VOLP:

Say, it was corrupted.

MOS:

I'll say it stunk, sir; and was fain to have it
Coffin'd up instantly, and sent away.

VOLP:

Any thing; what thou wilt. Hold, here's my will.
Get thee a cap, a count-book, pen and ink,
Papers afore thee; sit as thou wert taking
An inventory of parcels: I'll get up
Behind the curtain, on a stool, and hearken;
Sometime peep over, see how they do look,
With what degrees their blood doth leave their faces,
O, 'twill afford me a rare meal of laughter!

MOS *[PUTTING ON A CAP, AND SETTING OUT THE TABLE, ETC.]:*

Your advocate will turn stark dull upon it.
VOLP:
It will take off his oratory's edge.
MOS:
But your clarissimo, old round-back, he
Will crump you like a hog-louse, with the touch.
VOLP:
And what Corvino?
MOS:
O, sir, look for him,
To-morrow morning, with a rope and dagger,
To visit all the streets; he must run mad.
My lady too, that came into the court,
To bear false witness for your worship--
VOLP:
Yes,
And kist me 'fore the fathers; when my face
Flow'd all with oils.
MOS:
And sweat, sir. Why, your gold
Is such another med'cine, it dries up
All those offensive savours: it transforms
The most deformed, and restores them lovely,
As 'twere the strange poetical girdle. Jove
Could not invent t' himself a shroud more subtle
To pass Acrisius' guards. It is the thing
Makes all the world her grace, her youth, her beauty.
VOLP:
I think she loves me.
MOS:
Who? the lady, sir?
She's jealous of you.
VOLP:
Dost thou say so?

[KNOCKING WITHIN.]

MOS:
Hark,
There's some already.
VOLP:
Look.
MOS:
It is the Vulture:
He has the quickest scent.
VOLP:
I'll to my place,
Thou to thy posture.

[GOES BEHIND THE CURTAIN.]

MOS:
I am set.
VOLP:
But,Mosca,
Play the artificer now, torture them rarely.

[ENTER VOLTORE.]

VOLT:
How now, my Mosca?
MOS *[WRITING.]:*
"Turkey carpets, nine"--
VOLT:
Taking an inventory! that is well.
MOS:
"Two suits of bedding, tissue"--
VOLT:
Where's the Will?

Let me read that the while.

[ENTER SERVANTS, WITH CORBACCIO IN A CHAIR.]

CORB:
So, set me down:
And get you home.

[EXEUNT SERVANTS.]

VOLT:
Is he come now, to trouble us!
MOS:
"Of cloth of gold, two more"--
CORB:
Is it done, Mosca?
MOS:
"Of several velvets, eight"--
VOLT:
I like his care.
CORB:
Dost thou not hear?

[ENTER CORVINO.]

CORB:
Ha! is the hour come, Mosca?
VOLP *[PEEPING OVER THE CURTAIN.]*:
Ay, now, they muster.
CORV:
What does the advocate here,
Or this Corbaccio?
CORB:
What do these here?

[ENTER LADY POL. WOULD-BE.]

LADY P:
Mosca!
Is his thread spun?
MOS:
"Eight chests of linen"--
VOLP:
O,
My fine dame Would-be, too!
CORV:
Mosca, the Will,
That I may shew it these, and rid them hence.
MOS:
"Six chests of diaper, four of damask."--There.

[GIVES THEM THE WILL CARELESSLY, OVER HIS SHOULDER.]

CORB:
Is that the will?
MOS:
"Down-beds, and bolsters"--
VOLP:
Rare!
Be busy still. Now they begin to flutter:
They never think of me. Look, see, see, see!
How their swift eyes run over the long deed,
Unto the name, and to the legacies,
What is bequeath'd them there--
MOS:
"Ten suits of hangings"--
VOLP:
Ay, in their garters, Mosca. Now their hopes
Are at the gasp.

VOLT:

Mosca the heir?

CORB:

What's that?

VOLP:

My advocate is dumb; look to my merchant,
He has heard of some strange storm, a ship is lost,
He faints; my lady will swoon. Old glazen eyes,
He hath not reach'd his despair yet.

CORB *[TAKES THE WILL.]:*

All these
Are out of hope: I am sure, the man.

CORV:

But, Mosca--

MOS:

"Two cabinets."

CORV:

Is this in earnest?

MOS:

"One
Of ebony"--

CORV:

Or do you but delude me?

MOS:

The other, mother of pearl--I am very busy.
Good faith, it is a fortune thrown upon me--
"Item, one salt of agate"--not my seeking.

LADY P:

Do you hear, sir?

MOS:

"A perfum'd box"--'Pray you forbear,
You see I'm troubled--"made of an onyx"--

LADY P:

How!

MOS:

To-morrow or next day, I shall be at leisure
To talk with you all.
CORV:

Is this my large hope's issue?
LADY P:

Sir, I must have a fairer answer.
MOS:

Madam!
Marry, and shall: 'pray you, fairly quit my house.
Nay, raise no tempest with your looks; but hark you,
Remember what your ladyship offer'd me,
To put you in an heir; go to, think on it:
And what you said e'en your best madams did
For maintenance, and why not you? Enough.
Go home, and use the poor sir Pol, your knight, well,
For fear I tell some riddles; go, be melancholy.

[EXIT LADY WOULD-BE.]

VOLP:

O, my fine devil!
CORV:

Mosca, 'pray you a word.
MOS:

Lord! will you not take your dispatch hence yet?
Methinks, of all, you should have been the example.
Why should you stay here? with what thought? what prom-
ise?
Hear you; do not you know, I know you an ass,
And that you would most fain have been a wittol,
If fortune would have let you? that you are
A declared cuckold, on good terms? This pearl,
You'll say, was yours? right: this diamond?
I'll not deny't, but thank you. Much here else?

It may be so. Why, think that these good works
May help to hide your bad. I'll not betray you;
Although you be but extraordinary,
And have it only in title, it sufficeth:
Go home, be melancholy too, or mad.

[EXIT CORVINO.]

VOLP:
Rare Mosca! how his villany becomes him!
VOLT:
Certain he doth delude all these for me.
CORB:
Mosca the heir!
VOLP:
O, his four eyes have found it.
CORB:
I am cozen'd, cheated, by a parasite slave;
Harlot, thou hast gull'd me.
MOS:
Yes, sir. Stop your mouth,
Or I shall draw the only tooth is left.
Are not you he, that filthy covetous wretch,
With the three legs, that, here, in hope of prey,
Have, any time this three years, snuff'd about,
With your most grovelling nose; and would have hired
Me to the poisoning of my patron, sir?
Are not you he that have to-day in court
Profess'd the disinheriting of your son?
Perjured yourself? Go home, and die, and stink.
If you but croak a syllable, all comes out:
Away, and call your porters!
[exit corbaccio.]
Go, go, stink.
VOLP:

Excellent varlet!
VOLT:
Now, my faithful Mosca,
I find thy constancy.
MOS:
Sir!
VOLT:
Sincere.
MOS [WRITING.]:
"A table
Of porphyry"--I marle, you'll be thus troublesome.
VOLP:
Nay, leave off now, they are gone.
MOS:
Why? who are you?
What! who did send for you? O, cry you mercy,
Reverend sir! Good faith, I am grieved for you,
That any chance of mine should thus defeat
Your (I must needs say) most deserving travails:
But I protest, sir, it was cast upon me,
And I could almost wish to be without it,
But that the will o' the dead must be observ'd,
Marry, my joy is that you need it not,
You have a gift, sir, (thank your education,)
Will never let you want, while there are men,
And malice, to breed causes. Would I had
But half the like, for all my fortune, sir!
If I have any suits, as I do hope,
Things being so easy and direct, I shall not,
I will make bold with your obstreperous aid,
Conceive me,--for your fee, sir. In mean time,
You that have so much law, I know have the conscience,
Not to be covetous of what is mine.
Good sir, I thank you for my plate; 'twill help

To set up a young man. Good faith, you look
As you were costive; best go home and purge, sir.

[EXIT VOLTORE.]

VOLP

[COMES FROM BEHIND THE CURTAIN.]:
Bid him eat lettuce well.
My witty mischief,
Let me embrace thee. O that I could now
Transform thee to a Venus!--Mosca, go,
Straight take my habit of clarissimo,
And walk the streets; be seen, torment them more:
We must pursue, as well as plot. Who would
Have lost this feast?

MOS:

I doubt it will lose them.

VOLP:

O, my recovery shall recover all.
That I could now but think on some disguise
To meet them in, and ask them questions:
How I would vex them still at every turn!

MOS:

Sir, I can fit you.

VOLP:

Canst thou?

MOS:

Yes, I know
One o' the commandadori, sir, so like you;
Him will I straight make drunk, and bring you his habit.

VOLP:

A rare disguise, and answering thy brain!
O, I will be a sharp disease unto them.

MOS:

Sir, you must look for curses--

VOLP:

Till they burst;
The Fox fares ever best when he is curst.

[EXEUNT.]

SCENE 5.2.

A HALL IN SIR POLITICK'S HOUSE.

ENTER PEREGRINE DISGUISED, AND THREE MERCHANTS.

PER:

Am I enough disguised?

1 MER:

I warrant you.

PER:

All my ambition is to fright him only.

2 MER:

If you could ship him away, 'twere excellent.

3 MER:

To Zant, or to Aleppo?

PER:

Yes, and have his
Adventures put i' the Book of Voyages.
And his gull'd story register'd for truth.
Well, gentlemen, when I am in a while,
And that you think us warm in our discourse,
Know your approaches.

1 MER:

Trust it to our care.

[EXEUNT MERCHANTS.]

[ENTER WAITING-WOMAN.]

PER:
Save you, fair lady! Is sir Pol within?
WOM:
I do not know, sir.
PER:
Pray you say unto him,
Here is a merchant, upon earnest business,
Desires to speak with him.
WOM:
I will see, sir.

[EXIT.]

PER:
Pray you.--
I see the family is all female here.

[RE-ENTER WAITING-WOMAN.]

WOM:
He says, sir, he has weighty affairs of state,
That now require him whole; some other time
You may possess him.
PER:
Pray you say again,
If those require him whole, these will exact him,
Whereof I bring him tidings.

[EXIT WOMAN.]

--What might be
His grave affair of state now! how to make
Bolognian sausages here in Venice, sparing

One o' the ingredients?

[RE-ENTER WAITING-WOMAN.]

WOM:
Sir, he says, he knows
By your word "tidings," that you are no statesman,
And therefore wills you stay.
PER:
Sweet, pray you return him;
I have not read so many proclamations,
And studied them for words, as he has done--
But--here he deigns to come.

[EXIT WOMAN.]

[ENTER SIR POLITICK.]

SIR P:
Sir, I must crave
Your courteous pardon. There hath chanced to-day,
Unkind disaster 'twixt my lady and me;
And I was penning my apology,
To give her satisfaction, as you came now.
PER:
Sir, I am grieved I bring you worse disaster:
The gentleman you met at the port to-day,
That told you, he was newly arrived--
SIR P:
Ay, was
A fugitive punk?
PER:
No, sir, a spy set on you;
And he has made relation to the senate,

That you profest to him to have a plot
To sell the State of Venice to the Turk.
SIR P:
O me!
PER:
For which, warrants are sign'd by this time,
To apprehend you, and to search your study
For papers--
SIR P:
Alas, sir, I have none, but notes
Drawn out of play-books--
PER:
All the better, sir.
SIR P:
And some essays. What shall I do?
PER:
Sir, best
Convey yourself into a sugar-chest;
Or, if you could lie round, a frail were rare:
And I could send you aboard.
SIR P:
Sir, I but talk'd so,
For discourse sake merely.

[KNOCKING WITHIN.]

PER:
Hark! they are there.
SIR P:
I am a wretch, a wretch!
PER:
What will you do, sir?
Have you ne'er a currant-butt to leap into?
They'll put you to the rack, you must be sudden.
SIR P:

Sir, I have an ingine--
3 MER *[WITHIN.]:*
Sir Politick Would-be?
2 MER *[WITHIN.]:*
Where is he?
SIR P:
That I have thought upon before time.
PER:
What is it?
SIR P:
I shall ne'er endure the torture.
Marry, it is, sir, of a tortoise-shell,
Fitted for these extremities: pray you, sir, help me.
Here I've a place, sir, to put back my legs,
Please you to lay it on, sir,

[LIES DOWN WHILE PEREGRINE PLACES THE SHELL UPON HIM.]

--with this cap,
And my black gloves. I'll lie, sir, like a tortoise,
'Till they are gone.
PER:
And call you this an ingine?
SIR P:
Mine own device--Good sir, bid my wife's women
To burn my papers.

[EXIT PEREGRINE.]

[THE THREE MERCHANTS RUSH IN.]

1 MER:
Where is he hid?
3 MER:

We must,
And will sure find him.
2 MER:
Which is his study?

[RE-ENTER PEREGRINE.]

1 MER:
What
Are you, sir?
PER:
I am a merchant, that came here
To look upon this tortoise.
3 MER:
How!
1 MER:
St. Mark!
What beast is this!
PER:
It is a fish.
2 MER:
Come out here!
PER:
Nay, you may strike him, sir, and tread upon him;
He'll bear a cart.
1 MER:
What, to run over him?
PER:
Yes, sir.
3 MER:
Let's jump upon him.
2 MER:
Can he not go?
PER:
He creeps, sir.

1 MER:

Let's see him creep.

PER:

No, good sir, you will hurt him.

2 MER:

Heart, I will see him creep, or prick his guts.

3 MER:

Come out here!

PER:

Pray you, sir!

[ASIDE TO SIR POLITICK.]

--Creep a little.

1 MER:

Forth.

2 MER:

Yet farther.

PER:

Good sir!--Creep.

2 MER:

We'll see his legs.

[THEY PULL OFF THE SHELL AND DISCOVER HIM.]

3 MER:

Ods so, he has garters!

1 MER:

Ay, and gloves!

2 MER:

Is this

Your fearful tortoise?

PER *[DISCOVERING HIMSELF.]*:

Now, sir Pol, we are even;

For your next project I shall be prepared:
I am sorry for the funeral of your notes, sir.

1 MER:

'Twere a rare motion to be seen in Fleet-street.

2 MER:

Ay, in the Term.

1 MER:

Or Smithfield, in the fair.

3 MER:

Methinks 'tis but a melancholy sight.

PER:

Farewell, most politic tortoise!

[EXEUNT PER. AND MERCHANTS.]

[RE-ENTER WAITING-WOMAN.]

SIR P:

Where's my lady?
Knows she of this?

WOM:

I know not, sir.

SIR P:

Enquire.--
O, I shall be the fable of all feasts,
The freight of the gazetti; ship-boy's tale;
And, which is worst, even talk for ordinaries.

WOM:

My lady's come most melancholy home,
And says, sir, she will straight to sea, for physic.

SIR P:

And I to shun this place and clime for ever;
Creeping with house on back: and think it well,
To shrink my poor head in my politic shell.

[EXEUNT.]

SCENE 5.3.

A ROOM IN VOLPONE'S HOUSE.

ENTER MOSCA IN THE HABIT OF A CLARISSIMO; AND VOLPONE IN THAT OF A COMMANDADORE.

VOLP:
Am I then like him?
MOS:
O, sir, you are he;
No man can sever you.
VOLP:
Good.
MOS:
But what am I?
VOLP:
'Fore heaven, a brave clarissimo, thou becom'st it!
Pity thou wert not born one.
MOS *[ASIDE.]*:
If I hold
My made one, 'twill be well.
VOLP:
I'll go and see
What news first at the court.

[EXIT.]

MOS:
Do so. My Fox
Is out of his hole, and ere he shall re-enter,
I'll make him languish in his borrow'd case,

Except he come to composition with me.--
Androgyno, Castrone, Nano!

[ENTER ANDROGYNO, CASTRONE AND NANO.]

ALL:
Here.
MOS:
Go, recreate yourselves abroad; go sport.--

[EXEUNT.]

So, now I have the keys, and am possest.
Since he will needs be dead afore his time,
I'll bury him, or gain by him: I am his heir,
And so will keep me, till he share at least.
To cozen him of all, were but a cheat
Well placed; no man would construe it a sin:
Let his sport pay for it, this is call'd the Fox-trap.

[EXIT.]

SCENE 5.4

A STREET.

ENTER CORBACCIO AND CORVINO.

CORB:
They say, the court is set.
CORV:
We must maintain
Our first tale good, for both our reputations.
CORB:

Why, mine's no tale: my son would there have kill'd me.

CORV:

That's true, I had forgot:--

[ASIDE.]--mine is, I am sure.

But for your Will, sir.

CORB:

Ay, I'll come upon him

For that hereafter; now his patron's dead.

[ENTER VOLPONE.]

VOLP:

Signior Corvino! and Corbaccio! sir,

Much joy unto you.

CORV:

Of what?

VOLP:

The sudden good,

Dropt down upon you--

CORB:

Where?

VOLP:

And, none knows how,

From old Volpone, sir.

CORB:

Out, arrant knave!

VOLP:

Let not your too much wealth, sir, make you furious.

CORB:

Away, thou varlet!

VOLP:

Why, sir?

CORB:

Dost thou mock me?

VOLP:

You mock the world, sir; did you not change Wills?

CORB:

Out, harlot!

VOLP:

O! belike you are the man,
Signior Corvino? 'faith, you carry it well;
You grow not mad withal: I love your spirit:
You are not over-leaven'd with your fortune.
You should have some would swell now, like a wine-fat,
With such an autumn--Did he give you all, sir?

CORB:

Avoid, you rascal!

VOLP:

Troth, your wife has shewn
Herself a very woman; but you are well,
You need not care, you have a good estate,
To bear it out sir, better by this chance:
Except Corbaccio have a share.

CORV:

Hence, varlet.

VOLP:

You will not be acknown, sir; why, 'tis wise.
Thus do all gamesters, at all games, dissemble:
No man will seem to win.
[exeunt corvino and corbaccio.]
--Here comes my vulture,
Heaving his beak up in the air, and snuffing.

[ENTER VOLTORE.]

VOLT:

Outstript thus, by a parasite! a slave,
Would run on errands, and make legs for crumbs?
Well, what I'll do--

VOLP:

>The court stays for your worship.
>I e'en rejoice, sir, at your worship's happiness,
>And that it fell into so learned hands,
>That understand the fingering--

VOLT:

>What do you mean?

VOLP:

>I mean to be a suitor to your worship,
>For the small tenement, out of reparations,
>That, to the end of your long row of houses,
>By the Piscaria: it was, in Volpone's time,
>Your predecessor, ere he grew diseased,
>A handsome, pretty, custom'd bawdy-house,
>As any was in Venice, none dispraised;
>But fell with him; his body and that house
>Decay'd, together.

VOLT:

>Come sir, leave your prating.

VOLP:

>Why, if your worship give me but your hand,
>That I may have the refusal, I have done.
>'Tis a mere toy to you, sir; candle-rents;
>As your learn'd worship knows--

VOLT:

>What do I know?

VOLP:

>Marry, no end of your wealth, sir, God decrease it!

VOLT:

>Mistaking knave! what, mockst thou my misfortune?

[EXIT.]

VOLP:

His blessing on your heart, sir; would 'twere more!--
Now to my first again, at the next corner.

[EXIT.]

SCENE 5.5.

ANOTHER PART OF THE STREET.

*ENTER CORBACCIO AND CORVINO;-- MOSCA PASSES OVER THE
STAGE, BEFORE THEM.*

CORB:
See, in our habit! see the impudent varlet!
CORV:
That I could shoot mine eyes at him like gun-stones.

[ENTER VOLPONE.]

VOLP:
But is this true, sir, of the parasite?
CORB:
Again, to afflict us! monster!
VOLP:
In good faith, sir,
I'm heartily grieved, a beard of your grave length
Should be so over-reach'd. I never brook'd
That parasite's hair; methought his nose should cozen:
There still was somewhat in his look, did promise
The bane of a clarissimo.
CORB:
Knave--
VOLP:
Methinks
Yet you, that are so traded in the world,

A witty merchant, the fine bird, Corvino,
That have such moral emblems on your name,
Should not have sung your shame; and dropt your cheese,
To let the Fox laugh at your emptiness.

CORV:

Sirrah, you think the privilege of the place,
And your red saucy cap, that seems to me
Nail'd to your jolt-head with those two chequines,
Can warrant your abuses; come you hither:
You shall perceive, sir, I dare beat you; approach.

VOLP:

No haste, sir, I do know your valour well,
Since you durst publish what you are, sir.

CORV:

Tarry,
I'd speak with you.

VOLP:

Sir, sir, another time--

CORV:

Nay, now.

VOLP:

O lord, sir! I were a wise man,
Would stand the fury of a distracted cuckold.

[AS HE IS RUNNING OFF, RE-ENTER MOSCA.]

CORB:

What, come again!

VOLP:

Upon 'em, Mosca; save me.

CORB:

The air's infected where he breathes.

CORV:

Let's fly him.

[EXEUNT CORV. AND CORB.]

VOLP:

Excellent basilisk! turn upon the vulture.

[ENTER VOLTORE.]

VOLT:

Well, flesh-fly, it is summer with you now;
Your winter will come on.

MOS:

Good advocate,
Prithee not rail, nor threaten out of place thus;
Thou'lt make a solecism, as madam says.
Get you a biggin more, your brain breaks loose.

[EXIT.]

VOLT:

Well, sir.

VOLP:

Would you have me beat the insolent slave,
Throw dirt upon his first good clothes?

VOLT:

This same
Is doubtless some familiar.

VOLP:

Sir, the court,
In troth, stays for you. I am mad, a mule
That never read Justinian, should get up,
And ride an advocate. Had you no quirk
To avoid gullage, sir, by such a creature?
I hope you do but jest; he has not done it:
'Tis but confederacy, to blind the rest.

You are the heir.
VOLT:
A strange, officious,
Troublesome knave! thou dost torment me.
VOLP:
I know--
It cannot be, sir, that you should be cozen'd;
'Tis not within the wit of man to do it;
You are so wise, so prudent; and 'tis fit
That wealth and wisdom still should go together.

[EXEUNT.]

SCENE 5.6.

THE SCRUTINEO OR SENATE-HOUSE.

ENTER AVOCATORI, NOTARIO, BONARIO, CELIA, CORBACCIO, CORVINO, COMMANDADORI, SAFFI, ETC.

1 AVOC:
Are all the parties here?
NOT:
All but the advocate.
2 AVOC:
And here he comes.

[ENTER VOLTORE AND VOLPONE.]

1 AVOC:
Then bring them forth to sentence.
VOLT:
O, my most honour'd fathers, let your mercy
Once win upon your justice, to forgive--

I am distracted--
VOLP *[ASIDE.]*:
What will he do now?
VOLT:
O,
I know not which to address myself to first;
Whether your fatherhoods, or these innocents--
CORV *[ASIDE.]*:
Will he betray himself?
VOLT:
Whom equally
I have abused, out of most covetous ends--
CORV:
The man is mad!
CORB:
What's that?
CORV:
He is possest.
VOLT:
For which, now struck in conscience, here, I prostate
Myself at your offended feet, for pardon.
1, 2 AVOC:
Arise.
CEL:
O heaven, how just thou art!
VOLP *[ASIDE.]*:
I am caught
In mine own noose--
CORV *[TO CORBACCIO.]*:
Be constant, sir: nought now
Can help, but impudence.
1 AVOC:
Speak forward.
COM:
Silence!

VOLT:

It is not passion in me, reverend fathers,
But only conscience, conscience, my good sires,
That makes me now tell trueth. That parasite,
That knave, hath been the instrument of all.

1 AVOC:

Where is that knave? fetch him.

VOLP:

I go.

[EXIT.]

CORV:

Grave fathers,
This man's distracted; he confest it now:
For, hoping to be old Volpone's heir,
Who now is dead--

3 AVOC:

How?

2 AVOC:

Is Volpone dead?

CORV:

Dead since, grave fathers--

BON:

O sure vengeance!

1 AVOC:

Stay,
Then he was no deceiver?

VOLT:

O no, none:
The parasite, grave fathers.

CORV:

He does speak
Out of mere envy, 'cause the servant's made

The thing he gaped for: please your fatherhoods,
This is the truth, though I'll not justify
The other, but he may be some-deal faulty.
VOLT:
Ay, to your hopes, as well as mine, Corvino:
But I'll use modesty. Pleaseth your wisdoms,
To view these certain notes, and but confer them;
As I hope favour, they shall speak clear truth.
CORV:
The devil has enter'd him!
BON:
Or bides in you.
4 AVOC:
We have done ill, by a public officer,
To send for him, if he be heir.
2 AVOC:
For whom?
4 AVOC:
Him that they call the parasite.
3 1AVOC: 'Tis true,
He is a man of great estate, now left.
4 AVOC:
Go you, and learn his name, and say, the court
Entreats his presence here, but to the clearing
Of some few doubts.

[EXIT NOTARY.]

2 AVOC:
This same's a labyrinth!
1 AVOC:
Stand you unto your first report?
CORV:
My state,
My life, my fame--

BON:

Where is it?

CORV:

Are at the stake

1 AVOC:

Is yours so too?

CORB:

The advocate's a knave,
And has a forked tongue--

2 AVOC:

Speak to the point.

CORB:

So is the parasite too.

1 AVOC:

This is confusion.

VOLT:

I do beseech your fatherhoods, read but those--

[GIVING THEM THE PAPERS.]

CORV:

And credit nothing the false spirit hath writ:
It cannot be, but he's possest grave fathers.

[THE SCENE CLOSES.]

SCENE 5.7.

A STREET.

ENTER VOLPONE.

VOLP:

To make a snare for mine own neck! and run

My head into it, wilfully! with laughter!
When I had newly 'scaped, was free, and clear,
Out of mere wantonness! O, the dull devil
Was in this brain of mine, when I devised it,
And Mosca gave it second; he must now
Help to sear up this vein, or we bleed dead.--

[ENTER NANO, ANDROGYNO, AND CASTRONE.]

How now! who let you loose? whither go you now?
What, to buy gingerbread? or to drown kitlings?
NAN:
Sir, master Mosca call'd us out of doors,
And bid us all go play, and took the keys.
AND:
Yes.
VOLP:
Did master Mosca take the keys? why so!
I'm farther in. These are my fine conceits!
I must be merry, with a mischief to me!
What a vile wretch was I, that could not bear
My fortune soberly? I must have my crotchets,
And my conundrums! Well, go you, and seek him:
His meaning may be truer than my fear.
Bid him, he straight come to me to the court;
Thither will I, and, if't be possible,
Unscrew my advocate, upon new hopes:
When I provoked him, then I lost myself.

[EXEUNT.]

SCENE 5.8.

THE SCRUTINEO, OR SENATE-HOUSE.

AVOCATORI, BONARIO, CELIA, CORBACCIO, CORVINO, COMMANDADORI, SAFFI, ETC., AS BEFORE.

1 AVOC:

These things can ne'er be reconciled. He, here,

[SHEWING THE PAPERS.]

Professeth, that the gentleman was wrong'd,
And that the gentlewoman was brought thither,
Forced by her husband, and there left.

VOLT:

Most true.

CEL:

How ready is heaven to those that pray!

1 AVOC:

But that
Volpone would have ravish'd her, he holds
Utterly false; knowing his impotence.

CORV:

Grave fathers, he's possest; again, I say,
Possest: nay, if there be possession, and
Obsession, he has both.

3 AVOC:

Here comes our officer.

[ENTER VOLPONE.]

VOLP:

The parasite will straight be here, grave fathers.

4 AVOC:

You might invent some other name, sir varlet.

3 AVOC:

Did not the notary meet him?

VOLP:

Not that I know.

4 AVOC:

His coming will clear all.

2 AVOC:

Yet, it is misty.

VOLT:

May't please your fatherhoods--

VOLP *[whispers volt.]:*

Sir, the parasite

Will'd me to tell you, that his master lives;

That you are still the man; your hopes the same;

And this was only a jest--

VOLT:

How?

VOLP:

Sir, to try

If you were firm, and how you stood affected.

VOLT:

Art sure he lives?

VOLP:

Do I live, sir?

VOLT:

O me!

I was too violent.

VOLP:

Sir, you may redeem it,

They said, you were possest; fall down, and seem so:

I'll help to make it good.

[voltore falls.]

--God bless the man!--

Stop your wind hard, and swell: See, see, see, see!

He vomits crooked pins! his eyes are set,

Like a dead hare's hung in a poulter's shop!

His mouth's running away! Do you see, signior?

Now it is in his belly!

CORV:

Ay, the devil!

VOLP:

Now in his throat.

CORV:

Ay, I perceive it plain.

VOLP:

'Twill out, 'twill out! stand clear.

See, where it flies,

In shape of a blue toad, with a bat's wings!

Do you not see it, sir?

CORB:

What? I think I do.

CORV:

'Tis too manifest.

VOLP:

Look! he comes to himself!

VOLT:

Where am I?

VOLP:

Take good heart, the worst is past, sir.

You are dispossest.

1 AVOC:

What accident is this!

2 AVOC:

Sudden, and full of wonder!

3 AVOC:

If he were

Possest, as it appears, all this is nothing.

CORV:

He has been often subject to these fits.

1 AVOC:

Shew him that writing:--do you know it, sir?

VOLP

[WHISPERS VOLT.]:
Deny it, sir, forswear it; know it not.

VOLT:

Yes, I do know it well, it is my hand;
But all that it contains is false.

BON:

O practice!

2 AVOC:

What maze is this!

1 AVOC:

Is he not guilty then,
Whom you there name the parasite?

VOLT:

Grave fathers,
No more than his good patron, old Volpone.

4 AVOC:

Why, he is dead.

VOLT:

O no, my honour'd fathers,
He lives--

1 AVOC:

How! lives?

VOLT:

Lives.

2 AVOC:

This is subtler yet!

3 AVOC:

You said he was dead.

VOLT:

Never.

3 AVOC:

You said so.

CORV:

I heard so.

4 AVOC:

Here comes the gentleman; make him way.

[ENTER MOSCA.]

3 AVOC:

A stool.

4 AVOC *[ASIDE.]:*

A proper man; and, were Volpone dead,
A fit match for my daughter.

3 AVOC:

Give him way.

VOLP *[ASIDE TO MOSCA.]:*

Mosca, I was almost lost, the advocate
Had betrayed all; but now it is recovered;
All's on the hinge again--Say, I am living.

MOS:

What busy knave is this!--Most reverend fathers,
I sooner had attended your grave pleasures,
But that my order for the funeral
Of my dear patron, did require me--

VOLP *[ASIDE.]:*

Mosca!

MOS:

Whom I intend to bury like a gentleman.

VOLP *[ASIDE.]:*

Ay, quick, and cozen me of all.

2 AVOC:

Still stranger!
More intricate!

1 AVOC:

And come about again!

4 AVOC *[ASIDE.]:*

It is a match, my daughter is bestow'd.

MOS
> *[ASIDE TO VOLP.]:*
> Will you give me half?

VOLP:
> First, I'll be hang'd.

MOS:
> I know,
> Your voice is good, cry not so loud.

1 AVOC:
> Demand
> The advocate.--Sir, did not you affirm,
> Volpone was alive?

VOLP:
> Yes, and he is;
> This gentleman told me so.

[ASIDE TO VOLP.]

> --Thou shalt have half.--

MOS:
> Whose drunkard is this same? speak, some that know him:
> I never saw his face.

[ASIDE TO VOLP.]

> --I cannot now
> Afford it you so cheap.

VOLP:
> No!

1 AVOC:
> What say you?

VOLT:
> The officer told me.

VOLP:
> I did, grave fathers,

And will maintain he lives, with mine own life.
And that this creature
[POINTS TO MOSCA.] told me.
[ASIDE.]
--I was born,
With all good stars my enemies.

MOS:
Most grave fathers,
If such an insolence as this must pass
Upon me, I am silent: 'twas not this
For which you sent, I hope.

2 AVOC:
Take him away.

VOLP:
Mosca!

3 AVOC:
Let him be whipt.

VOLP:
Wilt thou betray me?
Cozen me?

3 AVOC:
And taught to bear himself
Toward a person of his rank.

4 AVOC:
Away.

[THE OFFICERS SEIZE VOLPONE.]

MOS:
I humbly thank your fatherhoods.

VOLP *[ASIDE.]*:
Soft, soft: Whipt!
And lose all that I have! If I confess,
It cannot be much more.

4 AVOC:

Sir, are you married?

VOLP:

They will be allied anon; I must be resolute:
The Fox shall here uncase.

[THROWS OFF HIS DISGUISE.]

MOS:

Patron!

VOLP:

Nay, now,
My ruins shall not come alone; your match
I'll hinder sure: my substance shall not glue you,
Nor screw you into a family.

MOS:

Why, patron!

VOLP:

I am Volpone, and this is my knave; *[POINTING TO MOSCA.]*
This *[TO VOLT.],* his own knave; This *[TO CORB.],* avarice's
fool;
This *[TO CORV.],* a chimera of wittol, fool, and knave:
And, reverend fathers, since we all can hope
Nought but a sentence, let's not now dispair it.
You hear me brief.

CORV:

May it please your fatherhoods--

COM:

Silence.

1 AVOC:

The knot is now undone by miracle.

2 AVOC:

Nothing can be more clear.

3 AVOC:

Or can more prove

These innocent.

1 AVOC:

Give them their liberty.

BON:

Heaven could not long let such gross crimes be hid.

2 AVOC:

If this be held the high-way to get riches,
May I be poor!

3 AVOC:

This is not the gain, but torment.

1 AVOC:

These possess wealth, as sick men possess fevers,
Which trulier may be said to possess them.

2 AVOC:

Disrobe that parasite.

CORV, MOS:

Most honour'd fathers!--

1 AVOC:

Can you plead aught to stay the course of justice?
If you can, speak.

CORV, VOLT:

We beg favour,

CEL:

And mercy.

1 AVOC:

You hurt your innocence, suing for the guilty.
Stand forth; and first the parasite: You appear
T'have been the chiefest minister, if not plotter,
In all these lewd impostures; and now, lastly,
Have with your impudence abused the court,
And habit of a gentleman of Venice,
Being a fellow of no birth or blood:
For which our sentence is, first, thou be whipt;
Then live perpetual prisoner in our gallies.

VOLT:

I thank you for him.

MOS:

Bane to thy wolvish nature!

1 AVOC:

Deliver him to the saffi.

[*MOSCA IS CARRIED OUT.*]

--Thou, Volpone,

By blood and rank a gentleman, canst not fall

Under like censure; but our judgment on thee

Is, that thy substance all be straight confiscate

To the hospital of the Incurabili:

And, since the most was gotten by imposture,

By feigning lame, gout, palsy, and such diseases,

Thou art to lie in prison, cramp'd with irons,

Till thou be'st sick, and lame indeed.--Remove him.

[*HE IS TAKEN FROM THE BAR.*]

VOLP:

This is call'd mortifying of a Fox.

1 AVOC:

Thou, Voltore, to take away the scandal

Thou hast given all worthy men of thy profession,

Art banish'd from their fellowship, and our state.

Corbaccio!--bring him near--We here possess

Thy son of all thy state, and confine thee

To the monastery of San Spirito;

Where, since thou knewest not how to live well here,

Thou shalt be learn'd to die well.

CORB:

Ah! what said he?

AND:

You shall know anon, sir.

1 AVOC:

Thou, Corvino, shalt
Be straight embark'd from thine own house, and row'd
Round about Venice, through the grand canale,
Wearing a cap, with fair long asses' ears,
Instead of horns; and so to mount, a paper
Pinn'd on thy breast, to the Berlina--

CORV:

Yes,
And have mine eyes beat out with stinking fish,
Bruised fruit and rotten eggs--'Tis well. I am glad
I shall not see my shame yet.

1 AVOC:

And to expiate
Thy wrongs done to thy wife, thou art to send her
Home to her father, with her dowry trebled:
And these are all your judgments.

ALL:

Honour'd fathers.--

1 AVOC:

Which may not be revoked. Now you begin,
When crimes are done, and past, and to be punish'd,
To think what your crimes are: away with them.
Let all that see these vices thus rewarded,
Take heart and love to study 'em! Mischiefs feed
Like beasts, till they be fat, and then they bleed.

[EXEUNT.]

[VOLPONE COMES FORWARD.]

VOLPONE:

The seasoning of a play, is the applause.
Now, though the Fox be punish'd by the laws,
He yet doth hope, there is no suffering due,

For any fact which he hath done 'gainst you;
If there be, censure him; here he doubtful stands:
If not, fare jovially, and clap your hands.

[EXIT.]

GLOSSARY

ABATE, cast down, subdue.

ABHORRING, repugnant (to), at variance.

ABJECT, base, degraded thing, outcast.

ABRASE, smooth, blank.

ABSOLUTE(LY), faultless(ly).

ABSTRACTED, abstract, abstruse.

ABUSE, deceive, insult, dishonour, make ill use of.

ACATER, caterer.

ACATES, cates.

ACCEPTIVE, willing, ready to accept, receive.

ACCOMMODATE, fit, befitting. (The word was a fashionable one and used on all occasions. See "Henry IV.," pt. 2, iii. 4).

ACCOST, draw near, approach.

ACKNOWN, confessedly acquainted with.

ACME, full maturity.

ADALANTADO, lord deputy or governor of a Spanish province.

ADJECTION, addition.

ADMIRATION, astonishment.

ADMIRE, wonder, wonder at.

ADROP, philosopher's stone, or substance from which obtained.

ADSCRIVE, subscribe.

ADULTERATE, spurious, counterfeit.

ADVANCE, lift.

ADVERTISE, inform, give intelligence.

ADVERTISED, "be--," be it known to you.

ADVERTISEMENT, intelligence.

ADVISE, consider, bethink oneself, deliberate.

ADVISED, informed, aware; "are you--?" have you found that out?

AFFECT, love, like; aim at; move.

AFFECTED, disposed; beloved.

AFFECTIONATE, obstinate; prejudiced.

AFFECTS, affections.

AFFRONT, "give the--," face.
AFFY, have confidence in; betroth.
AFTER, after the manner of.
AGAIN, AGAINST, in anticipation of.
AGGRAVATE, increase, magnify, enlarge upon.
AGNOMINATION. See Paranomasie.
AIERY, nest, brood.
AIM, guess.
ALL HID, children's cry at hide-and-seek.
ALL-TO, completely, entirely ("all-to-be-laden").
ALLOWANCE, approbation, recognition.
ALMA-CANTARAS (astronomy), parallels of altitude.
ALMAIN, name of a dance.
ALMUTEN, planet of chief influence in the horoscope.
ALONE, unequalled, without peer.
ALUDELS, subliming pots.
AMAZED, confused, perplexed.
AMBER, AMBRE, ambergris.
AMBREE, MARY, a woman noted for her valour at the siege of Ghent, 1458.
AMES-ACE, lowest throw at dice.
AMPHIBOLIES, ambiguities.
AMUSED, bewildered, amazed.
AN, if.
ANATOMY, skeleton, or dissected body.
ANDIRONS, fire-dogs.
ANGEL, gold coin worth 10 shillings, stamped with the figure of the archangel Michael.
ANNESH CLEARE, spring known as Agnes le Clare.
ANSWER, return hit in fencing.
ANTIC, ANTIQUE, clown, buffoon.
ANTIC, like a buffoon.
ANTIPERISTASIS, an opposition which enhances the quality it opposes.
APOZEM, decoction.
APPERIL, peril.
APPLE-JOHN, APPLE-SQUIRE, pimp, pander.
APPLY, attach.
APPREHEND, take into custody.

APPREHENSIVE, quick of perception; able to perceive and appreciate.
APPROVE, prove, confirm.
APT, suit, adapt; train, prepare; dispose, incline.
APT(LY), suitable(y), opportune(ly).
APTITUDE, suitableness.
ARBOR, "make the--," cut up the game (Gifford).
ARCHES, Court of Arches.
ARCHIE, Archibald Armstrong, jester to James I. and Charles I.
ARGAILE, argol, crust or sediment in wine casks.
ARGENT-VIVE, quicksilver.
ARGUMENT, plot of a drama; theme, subject; matter in question; token, proof.
ARRIDE, please.
ARSEDINE, mixture of copper and zinc, used as an imitation of gold-leaf.
ARTHUR, PRINCE, reference to an archery show by a society who assumed arms, etc., of Arthur's knights.
ARTICLE, item.
ARTIFICIALLY, artfully.
ASCENSION, evaporation, distillation.
ASPIRE, try to reach, obtain, long for.
ASSALTO (Italian), assault.
ASSAY, draw a knife along the belly of the deer, a ceremony of the hunting-field.
ASSOIL, solve.
ASSURE, secure possession or reversion of.
ATHANOR, a digesting furnace, calculated to keep up a constant heat.
ATONE, reconcile.
ATTACH, attack, seize.
AUDACIOUS, having spirit and confidence.
AUTHENTIC(AL), of authority, authorised, trustworthy, genuine.
AVISEMENT, reflection, consideration.
AVOID, begone! get rid of.
AWAY WITH, endure.
AZOCH, Mercurius Philosophorum.
BABION, baboon.
BABY, doll.
BACK-SIDE, back premises.

BAFFLE, treat with contempt.
BAGATINE, Italian coin, worth about the third of a farthing.
BAIARD, horse of magic powers known to old romance.
BALDRICK, belt worn across the breast to support bugle, etc.
BALE (of dice), pair.
BALK, overlook, pass by, avoid.
BALLACE, ballast.
BALLOO, game at ball.
BALNEUM (BAIN MARIE), a vessel for holding hot water in which other vessels are stood for heating.
BANBURY, "brother of--," Puritan.
BANDOG, dog tied or chained up.
BANE, woe, ruin.
BANQUET, a light repast; dessert.
BARB, to clip gold.
BARBEL, fresh-water fish.
BARE, meer; bareheaded; it was "a particular mark of state and grandeur for the coachman to be uncovered" (Gifford).
BARLEY-BREAK, game somewhat similar to base.
BASE, game of prisoner's base.
BASES, richly embroidered skirt reaching to the knees, or lower.
BASILISK, fabulous reptile, believed to slay with its eye.
BASKET, used for the broken provision collected for prisoners.
BASON, basons, etc., were beaten by the attendant mob when bad characters were "carted."
BATE, be reduced; abate, reduce.
BATOON, baton, stick.
BATTEN, feed, grow fat.
BAWSON, badger.
BEADSMAN, prayer-man, one engaged to pray for another.
BEAGLE, small hound; fig. spy.
BEAR IN HAND, keep in suspense, deceive with false hopes.
BEARWARD, bear leader.
BEDPHERE. See Phere.
BEDSTAFF, (?) wooden pin in the side of the bedstead for supporting the bedclothes (Johnson); one of the sticks or "laths"; a stick used in making a bed.
BEETLE, heavy mallet.

BEG, "I'd--him," the custody of minors and idiots was begged for; likewise property fallen forfeit to the Crown ("your house had been begged").
BELL-MAN, night watchman.
BENJAMIN, an aromatic gum.
BERLINA, pillory.
BESCUMBER, defile.
BESLAVE, beslabber.
BESOGNO, beggar.
BESPAWLE, bespatter.
BETHLEHEM GABOR, Transylvanian hero, proclaimed King of Hungary.
BEVER, drinking.
BEVIS, SIR, knight of romance whose horse was equally celebrated.
BEWRAY, reveal, make known.
BEZANT, heraldic term: small gold circle.
BEZOAR'S STONE, a remedy known by this name was a supposed antidote to poison.
BID-STAND, highwayman.
BIGGIN, cap, similar to that worn by the Beguines; nightcap.
BILIVE (belive), with haste.
BILK, nothing, empty talk.
BILL, kind of pike.
BILLET, wood cut for fuel, stick.
BIRDING, thieving.
BLACK SANCTUS, burlesque hymn, any unholy riot.
BLANK, originally a small French coin.
BLANK, white.
BLANKET, toss in a blanket.
BLAZE, outburst of violence.
BLAZE, (her.) blazon; publish abroad.
BLAZON, armorial bearings; fig. all that pertains to good birth and breeding.
BLIN, "withouten--," without ceasing.
BLOW, puff up.
BLUE, colour of servants' livery, hence "--order," "--waiters."
BLUSHET, blushing one.
BOB, jest, taunt.
BOB, beat, thump.

BODGE, measure.

BODKIN, dagger, or other short, pointed weapon; long pin with which the women fastened up their hair.

BOLT, roll (of material).

BOLT, dislodge, rout out; sift (boulting-tub).

BOLT'S-HEAD, long, straight-necked vessel for distillation.

BOMBARD SLOPS, padded, puffed-out breeches.

BONA ROBA, "good, wholesome, plum-cheeked wench" (Johnson) -- not always used in compliment.

BONNY-CLABBER, sour butter-milk.

BOOKHOLDER, prompter.

BOOT, "to--," into the bargain; "no--," of no avail.

BORACHIO, bottle made of skin.

BORDELLO, brothel.

BORNE IT, conducted, carried it through.

BOTTLE (of hay), bundle, truss.

BOTTOM, skein or ball of thread; vessel.

BOURD, jest.

BOVOLI, snails or cockles dressed in the Italian manner (Gifford).

BOW-POT, flower vase or pot.

BOYS, "terrible--," "angry--," roystering young bucks. (See Nares).

BRABBLES (BRABBLESH), brawls.

BRACH, bitch.

BRADAMANTE, a heroine in "Orlando Furioso."

BRADLEY, ARTHUR OF, a lively character commemorated in ballads.

BRAKE, frame for confining a horse's feet while being shod, or strong curb or bridle; trap.

BRANCHED, with "detached sleeve ornaments, projecting from the shoulders of the gown" (Gifford).

BRANDISH, flourish of weapon.

BRASH, brace.

BRAVE, bravado, braggart speech.

BRAVE (adv.), gaily, finely (apparelled).

BRAVERIES, gallants.

BRAVERY, extravagant gaiety of apparel.

BRAVO, bravado, swaggerer.

BRAZEN-HEAD, speaking head made by Roger Bacon.

BREATHE, pause for relaxation; exercise.

BREATH UPON, speak dispraisingly of.
BREND, burn.
BRIDE-ALE, wedding feast.
BRIEF, abstract; (mus.) breve.
BRISK, smartly dressed.
BRIZE, breese, gadfly.
BROAD-SEAL, state seal.
BROCK, badger (term of contempt).
BROKE, transact business as a broker.
BROOK, endure, put up with.
BROUGHTON, HUGH, an English divine and Hebrew scholar.
BRUIT, rumour.
BUCK, wash.
BUCKLE, bend.
BUFF, leather made of buffalo skin, used for military and serjeants' coats, etc.
BUFO, black tincture.
BUGLE, long-shaped bead.
BULLED, (?) bolled, swelled.
BULLIONS, trunk hose.
BULLY, term of familiar endearment.
BUNGY, Friar Bungay, who had a familiar in the shape of a dog.
BURDEN, refrain, chorus.
BURGONET, closely-fitting helmet with visor.
BURGULLION, braggadocio.
BURN, mark wooden measures ("--ing of cans").
BURROUGH, pledge, security.
BUSKIN, half-boot, foot gear reaching high up the leg.
BUTT-SHAFT, barbless arrow for shooting at butts.
BUTTER, NATHANIEL ("Staple of News"), a compiler of general news. (See Cunningham).
BUTTERY-HATCH, half-door shutting off the buttery, where provisions and liquors were stored.
BUY, "he bought me," formerly the guardianship of wards could be bought.
BUZ, exclamation to enjoin silence.
BUZZARD, simpleton.
BY AND BY, at once.

BY(E), "on the __," incidentally, as of minor or secondary importance; at the side.
BY-CHOP, by-blow, bastard.
CADUCEUS, Mercury's wand.
CALIVER, light kind of musket.
CALLET, woman of ill repute.
CALLOT, coif worn on the wigs of our judges or serjeants-at-law (Gifford).
CALVERED, crimped, or sliced and pickled. (See Nares).
CAMOUCCIO, wretch, knave.
CAMUSED, flat.
CAN, knows.
CANDLE-RENT, rent from house property.
CANDLE-WASTER, one who studies late.
CANTER, sturdy beggar.
CAP OF MAINTENCE, an insignia of dignity, a cap of state borne before kings at their coronation; also an heraldic term.
CAPABLE, able to comprehend, fit to receive instruction, impression.
CAPANEUS, one of the "Seven against Thebes."
CARACT, carat, unit of weight for precious stones, etc.; value, worth.
CARANZA, Spanish author of a book on duelling.
CARCANET, jewelled ornament for the neck.
CARE, take care; object.
CAROSH, coach, carriage.
CARPET, table-cover.
CARRIAGE, bearing, behaviour.
CARWHITCHET, quip, pun.
CASAMATE, casemate, fortress.
CASE, a pair.
CASE, "in--," in condition.
CASSOCK, soldier's loose overcoat.
CAST, flight of hawks, couple.
CAST, throw dice; vomit; forecast, calculate.
CAST, cashiered.
CASTING-GLASS, bottle for sprinkling perfume.
CASTRIL, kestrel, falcon.
CAT, structure used in sieges.
CATAMITE, old form of "ganymede."

CATASTROPHE, conclusion.
CATCHPOLE, sheriff's officer.
CATES, dainties, provisions.
CATSO, rogue, cheat.
CAUTELOUS, crafty, artful.
CENSURE, criticism; sentence.
CENSURE, criticise; pass sentence, doom.
CERUSE, cosmetic containing white lead.
CESS, assess.
CHANGE, "hunt--," follow a fresh scent.
CHAPMAN, retail dealer.
CHARACTER, handwriting.
CHARGE, expense.
CHARM, subdue with magic, lay a spell on, silence.
CHARMING, exercising magic power.
CHARTEL, challenge.
CHEAP, bargain, market.
CHEAR, CHEER, comfort, encouragement; food, entertainment.
CHECK AT, aim reproof at.
CHEQUIN, gold Italian coin.
CHEVRIL, from kidskin, which is elastic and pliable.
CHIAUS, Turkish envoy; used for a cheat, swindler.
CHILDERMASS DAY, Innocents' Day.
CHOKE-BAIL, action which does not allow of bail.
CHRYSOPOEIA, alchemy.
CHRYSOSPERM, ways of producing gold.
CIBATION, adding fresh substances to supply the waste of evaporation.
CIMICI, bugs.
CINOPER, cinnabar.
CIOPPINI, chopine, lady's high shoe.
CIRCLING BOY, "a species of roarer; one who in some way drew a man into a snare, to cheat or rob him" (Nares).
CIRCUMSTANCE, circumlocution, beating about the bush; ceremony, everything pertaining to a certain condition; detail, particular.
CITRONISE, turn citron colour.
CITTERN, kind of guitar.

CITY-WIRES, woman of fashion, who made use of wires for hair and dress.
CIVIL, legal.
CLAP, clack, chatter.
CLAPPER-DUDGEON, downright beggar.
CLAPS HIS DISH, a clap, or clack, dish (dish with a movable lid) was carried by beggars and lepers to show that the vessel was empty, and to give sound of their approach.
CLARIDIANA, heroine of an old romance.
CLARISSIMO, Venetian noble.
CLEM, starve.
CLICKET, latch.
CLIM O' THE CLOUGHS, etc., wordy heroes of romance.
CLIMATE, country.
CLOSE, secret, private; secretive.
CLOSENESS, secrecy.
CLOTH, arras, hangings.
CLOUT, mark shot at, bull's eye.
CLOWN, countryman, clodhopper.
COACH-LEAVES, folding blinds.
COALS, "bear no--," submit to no affront.
COAT-ARMOUR, coat of arms.
COAT-CARD, court-card.
COB-HERRING, HERRING-COB, a young herring.
COB-SWAN, male swan.
COCK-A-HOOP, denoting unstinted jollity; thought to be derived from turning on the tap that all might drink to the full of the flowing liquor.
COCKATRICE, reptile supposed to be produced from a cock's egg and to kill by its eye--used as a term of reproach for a woman.
COCK-BRAINED, giddy, wild.
COCKER, pamper.
COCKSCOMB, fool's cap.
COCKSTONE, stone said to be found in a cock's gizzard, and to possess particular virtues.
CODLING, softening by boiling.
COFFIN, raised crust of a pie.
COG, cheat, wheedle.
COIL, turmoil, confusion, ado.

COKELY, master of a puppet-show (Whalley).
COKES, fool, gull.
COLD-CONCEITED, having cold opinion of, coldly affected towards.
COLE-HARBOUR, a retreat for people of all sorts.
COLLECTION, composure; deduction.
COLLOP, small slice, piece of flesh.
COLLY, blacken.
COLOUR, pretext.
COLOURS, "fear no--," no enemy (quibble).
COLSTAFF, cowlstaff, pole for carrying a cowl=tub.
COME ABOUT, charge, turn round.
COMFORTABLE BREAD, spiced gingerbread.
COMING, forward, ready to respond, complaisant.
COMMENT, commentary; "sometime it is taken for a lie or fayned tale" (Bullokar, 1616).
COMMODITY, "current for--," allusion to practice of money-lenders, who forced the borrower to take part of the loan in the shape of worthless goods on which the latter had to make money if he could.
COMMUNICATE, share.
COMPASS, "in--," within the range, sphere.
COMPLEMENT, completion, completement; anything required for the perfecting or carrying out of a person or affair; accomplishment.
COMPLEXION, natural disposition, constitution.
COMPLIMENT, See Complement.
COMPLIMENTARIES, masters of accomplishments.
COMPOSITION, constitution; agreement, contract.
COMPOSURE, composition.
COMPTER, COUNTER, debtors' prison.
CONCEALMENT, a certain amount of church property had been retained at the dissolution of the monasteries; Elizabeth sent commissioners to search it out, and the courtiers begged for it.
CONCEIT, idea, fancy, witty invention, conception, opinion.
CONCEIT, apprehend.
CONCEITED, fancifully, ingeniously devised or conceived; possessed of intelligence, witty, ingenious (hence well conceited, etc.); disposed to joke; of opinion, possessed of an idea.
CONCEIVE, understand.
CONCENT, harmony, agreement.

CONCLUDE, infer, prove.
CONCOCT, assimilate, digest.
CONDEN'T, probably conducted.
CONDUCT, escort, conductor.
CONEY-CATCH, cheat.
CONFECT, sweetmeat.
CONFER, compare.
CONGIES, bows.
CONNIVE, give a look, wink, of secret intelligence.
CONSORT, company, concert.
CONSTANCY, fidelity, ardour, persistence.
CONSTANT, confirmed, persistent, faithful.
CONSTANTLY, firmly, persistently.
CONTEND, strive.
CONTINENT, holding together.
CONTROL (the point), bear or beat down.
CONVENT, assembly, meeting.
CONVERT, turn (oneself).
CONVEY, transmit from one to another.
CONVINCE, evince, prove; overcome, overpower; convict.
COP, head, top; tuft on head of birds; "a cop" may have reference to one or other meaning; Gifford and others interpret as "conical, terminating in a point."
COPE-MAN, chapman.
COPESMATE, companion.
COPY (Lat. copia), abundance, copiousness.
CORN ("powder--"), grain.
COROLLARY, finishing part or touch.
CORSIVE, corrosive.
CORTINE, curtain, (arch.) wall between two towers, etc.
CORYAT, famous for his travels, published as "Coryat's Crudities."
COSSET, pet lamb, pet.
COSTARD, head.
COSTARD-MONGER, apple-seller, coster-monger.
COSTS, ribs.
COTE, hut.
COTHURNAL, from "cothurnus," a particular boot worn by actors in Greek tragedy.

COTQUEAN, hussy.
COUNSEL, secret.
COUNTENANCE, means necessary for support; credit, standing.
COUNTER. See Compter.
COUNTER, pieces of metal or ivory for calculating at play.
COUNTER, "hunt--," follow scent in reverse direction.
COUNTERFEIT, false coin.
COUNTERPANE, one part or counterpart of a deed or indenture.
COUNTERPOINT, opposite, contrary point.
COURT-DISH, a kind of drinking-cup (Halliwell); N.E.D. quotes from Bp. Goodman's "Court of James I.": "The king...caused his carver to cut him out a court-dish, that is, something of every dish, which he sent him as part of his reversion," but this does not sound like short allowance or small receptacle.
COURT-DOR, fool.
COURTEAU, curtal, small horse with docked tail.
COURTSHIP, courtliness.
COVETISE, avarice.
COWSHARD, cow dung.
COXCOMB, fool's cap, fool.
COY, shrink; disdain.
COYSTREL, low varlet.
COZEN, cheat.
CRACK, lively young rogue, wag.
CRACK, crack up, boast; come to grief.
CRAMBE, game of crambo, in which the players find rhymes for a given word.
CRANCH, craunch.
CRANION, spider-like; also fairy appellation for a fly (Gifford, who refers to lines in Drayton's "Nimphidia").
CRIMP, game at cards.
CRINCLE, draw back, turn aside.
CRISPED, with curled or waved hair.
CROP, gather, reap.
CROPSHIRE, a kind of herring. (See N.E.D.)
CROSS, any piece of money, many coins being stamped with a cross.
CROSS AND PILE, heads and tails.
CROSSLET, crucible.

CROWD, fiddle.
CRUDITIES, undigested matter.
CRUMP, curl up.
CRUSADO, Portuguese gold coin, marked with a cross.
CRY ("he that cried Italian"), "speak in a musical cadence," intone, or declaim (?); cry up.
CUCKING-STOOL, used for the ducking of scolds, etc.
CUCURBITE, a gourd-shaped vessel used for distillation.
CUERPO, "in--," in undress.
CULLICE, broth.
CULLION, base fellow, coward.
CULLISEN, badge worn on their arm by servants.
CULVERIN, kind of cannon.
CUNNING, skill.
CUNNING, skilful.
CUNNING-MAN, fortune-teller.
CURE, care for.
CURIOUS(LY), scrupulous, particular; elaborate, elegant(ly), dainty(ly) (hence "in curious").
CURST, shrewish, mischievous.
CURTAL, dog with docked tail, of inferior sort.
CUSTARD, "quaking--," "--politic," reference to a large custard which formed part of a city feast and afforded huge entertainment, for the fool jumped into it, and other like tricks were played. (See "All's Well, etc." ii. 5, 40.)
CUTWORK, embroidery, open-work.
CYPRES (CYPRUS) (quibble), cypress (or cyprus) being a transparent material, and when black used for mourning.
DAGGER ("--frumety"), name of tavern.
DARGISON, apparently some person known in ballad or tale.
DAUPHIN MY BOY, refrain of old comic song.
DAW, daunt.
DEAD LIFT, desperate emergency.
DEAR, applied to that which in any way touches us nearly.
DECLINE, turn off from; turn away, aside.
DEFALK, deduct, abate.
DEFEND, forbid.
DEGENEROUS, degenerate.

DEGREES, steps.
DELATE, accuse.
DEMI-CULVERIN, cannon carrying a ball of about ten pounds.
DENIER, the smallest possible coin, being the twelfth part of a sou.
DEPART, part with.
DEPENDANCE, ground of quarrel in duello language.
DESERT, reward.
DESIGNMENT, design.
DESPERATE, rash, reckless.
DETECT, allow to be detected, betray, inform against.
DETERMINE, terminate.
DETRACT, draw back, refuse.
DEVICE, masque, show; a thing moved by wires, etc., puppet.
DEVISE, exact in every particular.
DEVISED, invented.
DIAPASM, powdered aromatic herbs, made into balls of perfumed paste. (See Pomander.)
DIBBLE, (?) moustache (N.E.D.); (?) dagger (Cunningham).
DIFFUSED, disordered, scattered, irregular.
DIGHT, dressed.
DILDO, refrain of popular songs; vague term of low meaning.
DIMBLE, dingle, ravine.
DIMENSUM, stated allowance.
DISBASE, debase.
DISCERN, distinguish, show a difference between.
DISCHARGE, settle for.
DISCIPLINE, reformation; ecclesiastical system.
DISCLAIM, renounce all part in.
DISCOURSE, process of reasoning, reasoning faculty.
DISCOURTSHIP, discourtesy.
DISCOVER, betray, reveal; display.
DISFAVOUR, disfigure.
DISPARAGEMENT, legal term applied to the unfitness in any way of a marriage arranged for in the case of wards.
DISPENSE WITH, grant dispensation for.
DISPLAY, extend.
DIS'PLE, discipline, teach by the whip.
DISPOSED, inclined to merriment.

DISPOSURE, disposal.
DISPRISE, depreciate.
DISPUNCT, not punctilious.
DISQUISITION, search.
DISSOLVED, enervated by grief.
DISTANCE, (?) proper measure.
DISTASTE, offence, cause of offence.
DISTASTE, render distasteful.
DISTEMPERED, upset, out of humour.
DIVISION (mus.), variation, modulation.
DOG-BOLT, term of contempt.
DOLE, given in dole, charity.
DOLE OF FACES, distribution of grimaces.
DOOM, verdict, sentence.
DOP, dip, low bow.
DOR, beetle, buzzing insect, drone, idler.
DOR, (?) buzz; "give the--," make a fool of.
DOSSER, pannier, basket.
DOTES, endowments, qualities.
DOTTEREL, plover; gull, fool.
DOUBLE, behave deceitfully.
DOXY, wench, mistress.
DRACHM, Greek silver coin.
DRESS, groom, curry.
DRESSING, coiffure.
DRIFT, intention.
DRYFOOT, track by mere scent of foot.
DUCKING, punishment for minor offences.
DUILL, grieve.
DUMPS, melancholy, originally a mournful melody.
DURINDANA, Orlando's sword.
DWINDLE, shrink away, be overawed.
EAN, yean, bring forth young.
EASINESS, readiness.
EBOLITION, ebullition.
EDGE, sword.
EECH, eke.
EGREGIOUS, eminently excellent.

EKE, also, moreover.

E-LA, highest note in the scale.

EGGS ON THE SPIT, important business on hand.

ELF-LOCK, tangled hair, supposed to be the work of elves.

EMMET, ant.

ENGAGE, involve.

ENGHLE. See Ingle.

ENGHLE, cajole; fondle.

ENGIN(E), device, contrivance; agent; ingenuity, wit.

ENGINER, engineer, deviser, plotter.

ENGINOUS, crafty, full of devices; witty, ingenious.

ENGROSS, monopolise.

ENS, an existing thing, a substance.

ENSIGNS, tokens, wounds.

ENSURE, assure.

ENTERTAIN, take into service.

ENTREAT, plead.

ENTREATY, entertainment.

ENTRY, place where a deer has lately passed.

ENVOY, denouement, conclusion.

ENVY, spite, calumny, dislike, odium.

EPHEMERIDES, calendars.

EQUAL, just, impartial.

ERECTION, elevation in esteem.

ERINGO, candied root of the sea-holly, formerly used as a sweetmeat and aphrodisiac.

ERRANT, arrant.

ESSENTIATE, become assimilated.

ESTIMATION, esteem.

ESTRICH, ostrich.

ETHNIC, heathen.

EURIPUS, flux and reflux.

EVEN, just equable.

EVENT, fate, issue.

EVENT(ED), issue(d).

EVERT, overturn.

EXACUATE, sharpen.

EXAMPLESS, without example or parallel.

EXCALIBUR, King Arthur's sword.
EXEMPLIFY, make an example of.
EXEMPT, separate, exclude.
EXEQUIES, obsequies.
EXHALE, drag out.
EXHIBITION, allowance for keep, pocket-money.
EXORBITANT, exceeding limits of propriety or law, inordinate.
EXORNATION, ornament.
EXPECT, wait.
EXPIATE, terminate.
EXPLICATE, explain, unfold.
EXTEMPORAL, extempore, unpremeditated.
EXTRACTION, essence.
EXTRAORDINARY, employed for a special or temporary purpose.
EXTRUDE, expel.
EYE, "in--," in view.
EYEBRIGHT, (?) a malt liquor in which the herb of this name was infused, or a person who sold the same (Gifford).
EYE-TINGE, least shade or gleam.
FACE, appearance.
FACES ABOUT, military word of command.
FACINOROUS, extremely wicked.
FACKINGS, faith.
FACT, deed, act, crime.
FACTIOUS, seditious, belonging to a party, given to party feeling.
FAECES, dregs.
FAGIOLI, French beans.
FAIN, forced, necessitated.
FAITHFUL, believing.
FALL, ruff or band turned back on the shoulders; or, veil.
FALSIFY, feign (fencing term).
FAME, report.
FAMILIAR, attendant spirit.
FANTASTICAL, capricious, whimsical.
FARCE, stuff.
FAR-FET. See Fet.
FARTHINGAL, hooped petticoat.
FAUCET, tapster.

FAULT, lack; loss, break in line of scent; "for--," in default of.
FAUTOR, partisan.
FAYLES, old table game similar to backgammon.
FEAR(ED), affright(ed).
FEAT, activity, operation; deed, action.
FEAT, elegant, trim.
FEE, "in--" by feudal obligation.
FEIZE, beat, belabour.
FELLOW, term of contempt.
FENNEL, emblem of flattery.
FERE, companion, fellow.
FERN-SEED, supposed to have power of rendering invisible.
FET, fetched.
FETCH, trick.
FEUTERER (Fr. vautrier), dog-keeper.
FEWMETS, dung.
FICO, fig.
FIGGUM, (?) jugglery.
FIGMENT, fiction, invention.
FIRK, frisk, move suddenly, or in jerks; "--up," stir up, rouse; "firks mad," suddenly behaves like a madman.
FIT, pay one out, punish.
FITNESS, readiness.
FITTON (FITTEN), lie, invention.
FIVE-AND-FIFTY, "highest number to stand on at primero" (Gifford).
FLAG, to fly low and waveringly.
FLAGON CHAIN, for hanging a smelling-bottle (Fr. flacon) round the neck (?). (See N.E.D.).
FLAP-DRAGON, game similar to snap-dragon.
FLASKET, some kind of basket.
FLAW, sudden gust or squall of wind.
FLAWN, custard.
FLEA, catch fleas.
FLEER, sneer, laugh derisively.
FLESH, feed a hawk or dog with flesh to incite it to the chase; initiate in blood-shed; satiate.
FLICKER-MOUSE, bat.
FLIGHT, light arrow.

FLITTER-MOUSE, bat.
FLOUT, mock, speak and act contemptuously.
FLOWERS, pulverised substance.
FLY, familiar spirit.
FOIL, weapon used in fencing; that which sets anything off to advantage.
FOIST, cut-purse, sharper.
FOND(LY), foolish(ly).
FOOT-CLOTH, housings of ornamental cloth which hung down on either side a horse to the ground.
FOOTING, foothold; footstep; dancing.
FOPPERY, foolery.
FOR, "--failing," for fear of failing.
FORBEAR, bear with; abstain from.
FORCE, "hunt at--," run the game down with dogs.
FOREHEAD, modesty; face, assurance, effrontery.
FORESLOW, delay.
FORESPEAK, bewitch; foretell.
FORETOP, front lock of hair which fashion required to be worn upright.
FORGED, fabricated.
FORM, state formally.
FORMAL, shapely; normal; conventional.
FORTHCOMING, produced when required.
FOUNDER, disable with over-riding.
FOURM, form, lair.
FOX, sword.
FRAIL, rush basket in which figs or raisins were packed.
FRAMPULL, peevish, sour-tempered.
FRAPLER, blusterer, wrangler.
FRAYING, "a stag is said to fray his head when he rubs it against a tree to...cause the outward coat of the new horns to fall off" (Gifford).
FREIGHT (of the gazetti), burden (of the newspapers).
FREQUENT, full.
FRICACE, rubbing.
FRICATRICE, woman of low character.
FRIPPERY, old clothes shop.
FROCK, smock-frock.

FROLICS, (?) humorous verses circulated at a feast (N.E.D.); couplets wrapped round sweetmeats (Cunningham).
FRONTLESS, shameless.
FROTED, rubbed.
FRUMETY, hulled wheat boiled in milk and spiced.
FRUMP, flout, sneer.
FUCUS, dye.
FUGEAND, (?) figent: fidgety, restless (N.E.D.).
FULLAM, false dice.
FULMART, polecat.
FULSOME, foul, offensive.
FURIBUND, raging, furious.
GALLEY-FOIST, city-barge, used on Lord Mayor's Day, when he was sworn into his office at Westminster (Whalley).
GALLIARD, lively dance in triple time.
GAPE, be eager after.
GARAGANTUA, Rabelais' giant.
GARB, sheaf (Fr. gerbe); manner, fashion, behaviour.
GARD, guard, trimming, gold or silver lace, or other ornament.
GARDED, faced or trimmed.
GARNISH, fee.
GAVEL-KIND, name of a land-tenure existing chiefly in Kent; from 16th century often used to denote custom of dividing a deceased man's property equally among his sons (N.E.D.).
GAZETTE, small Venetian coin worth about three-farthings.
GEANCE, jaunt, errand.
GEAR (GEER), stuff, matter, affair.
GELID, frozen.
GEMONIES, steps from which the bodies of criminals were thrown into the river.
GENERAL, free, affable.
GENIUS, attendant spirit.
GENTRY, gentlemen; manners characteristic of gentry, good breeding.
GIB-CAT, tom-cat.
GIGANTOMACHIZE, start a giants' war.
GIGLOT, wanton.
GIMBLET, gimlet.
GING, gang.

GLASS ("taking in of shadows, etc."), crystal or beryl.
GLEEK, card game played by three; party of three, trio; side glance.
GLICK (GLEEK), jest, gibe.
GLIDDER, glaze.
GLORIOUSLY, of vain glory.
GODWIT, bird of the snipe family.
GOLD-END-MAN, a buyer of broken gold and silver.
GOLL, hand.
GONFALIONIER, standard-bearer, chief magistrate, etc.
GOOD, sound in credit.
GOOD-YEAR, good luck.
GOOSE-TURD, colour of. (See Turd).
GORCROW, carrion crow.
GORGET, neck armour.
GOSSIP, godfather.
GOWKED, from "gowk," to stand staring and gaping like a fool.
GRANNAM, grandam.
GRASS, (?) grease, fat.
GRATEFUL, agreeable, welcome.
GRATIFY, give thanks to.
GRATITUDE, gratuity.
GRATULATE, welcome, congratulate.
GRAVITY, dignity.
GRAY, badger.
GRICE, cub.
GRIEF, grievance.
GRIPE, vulture, griffin.
GRIPE'S EGG, vessel in shape of.
GROAT, fourpence.
GROGRAN, coarse stuff made of silk and mohair, or of coarse silk.
GROOM-PORTER, officer in the royal household.
GROPE, handle, probe.
GROUND, pit (hence "grounded judgments").
GUARD, caution, heed.
GUARDANT, heraldic term: turning the head only.
GUILDER, Dutch coin worth about 4d.
GULES, gullet, throat; heraldic term for red.
GULL, simpleton, dupe.

GUST, taste.
HAB NAB, by, on, chance.
HABERGEON, coat of mail.
HAGGARD, wild female hawk; hence coy, wild.
HALBERD, combination of lance and battle-axe.
HALL, "a--!" a cry to clear the room for the dancers.
HANDSEL, first money taken.
HANGER, loop or strap on a sword-belt from which the sword was suspended.
HAP, fortune, luck.
HAPPILY, haply.
HAPPINESS, appropriateness, fitness.
HAPPY, rich.
HARBOUR, track, trace (an animal) to its shelter.
HARD-FAVOURED, harsh-featured.
HARPOCRATES, Horus the child, son of Osiris, figured with a finger pointing to his mouth, indicative of silence.
HARRINGTON, a patent was granted to Lord H. for the coinage of tokens (q.v.).
HARROT, herald.
HARRY NICHOLAS, founder of a community called the "Family of Love."
HAY, net for catching rabbits, etc.
HAY! (Ital. hai!), you have it (a fencing term).
HAY IN HIS HORN, ill-tempered person.
HAZARD, game at dice; that which is staked.
HEAD, "first--," young deer with antlers first sprouting; fig. a newly-ennobled man.
HEADBOROUGH, constable.
HEARKEN AFTER, inquire; "hearken out," find, search out.
HEARTEN, encourage.
HEAVEN AND HELL ("Alchemist"), names of taverns.
HECTIC, fever.
HEDGE IN, include.
HELM, upper part of a retort.
HER'NSEW, hernshaw, heron.
HIERONIMO (JERONIMO), hero of Kyd's "Spanish Tragedy."
HOBBY, nag.

HOBBY-HORSE, imitation horse of some light material, fastened round the waist of the morrice-dancer, who imitated the movements of a skittish horse.

HODDY-DODDY, fool.

HOIDEN, hoyden, formerly applied to both sexes (ancient term for leveret? Gifford).

HOLLAND, name of two famous chemists.

HONE AND HONERO, wailing expressions of lament or discontent.

HOOD-WINK'D, blindfolded.

HORARY, hourly.

HORN-MAD, stark mad (quibble).

HORN-THUMB, cut-purses were in the habit of wearing a horn shield on the thumb.

HORSE-BREAD-EATING, horses were often fed on coarse bread.

HORSE-COURSER, horse-dealer.

HOSPITAL, Christ's Hospital.

HOWLEGLAS, Eulenspiegel, the hero of a popular German tale which relates his buffooneries and knavish tricks.

HUFF, hectoring, arrogance.

HUFF IT, swagger.

HUISHER (Fr. huissier), usher.

HUM, beer and spirits mixed together.

HUMANITIAN, humanist, scholar.

HUMOROUS, capricious, moody, out of humour; moist.

HUMOUR, a word used in and out of season in the time of Shakespeare and Ben Jonson, and ridiculed by both.

HUMOURS, manners.

HUMPHREY, DUKE, those who were dinnerless spent the dinner-hour in a part of St. Paul's where stood a monument said to be that of the duke's; hence "dine with Duke Humphrey," to go hungry.

HURTLESS, harmless.

IDLE, useless, unprofitable.

ILL-AFFECTED, ill-disposed.

ILL-HABITED, unhealthy.

ILLUSTRATE, illuminate.

IMBIBITION, saturation, steeping.

IMBROCATA, fencing term: a thrust in tierce.

IMPAIR, impairment.

IMPART, give money.
IMPARTER, any one ready to be cheated and to part with his money.
IMPEACH, damage.
IMPERTINENCIES, irrelevancies.
IMPERTINENT(LY), irrelevant(ly), without reason or purpose.
IMPOSITION, duty imposed by.
IMPOTENTLY, beyond power of control.
IMPRESS, money in advance.
IMPULSION, incitement.
IN AND IN, a game played by two or three persons with four dice.
INCENSE, incite, stir up.
INCERATION, act of covering with wax; or reducing a substance to softness of wax.
INCH, "to their--es," according to their stature, capabilities.
INCH-PIN, sweet-bread.
INCONVENIENCE, inconsistency, absurdity.
INCONY, delicate, rare (used as a term of affection).
INCUBEE, incubus.
INCUBUS, evil spirit that oppresses us in sleep, nightmare.
INCURIOUS, unfastidious, uncritical.
INDENT, enter into engagement.
INDIFFERENT, tolerable, passable.
INDIGESTED, shapeless, chaotic.
INDUCE, introduce.
INDUE, supply.
INEXORABLE, relentless.
INFANTED, born, produced.
INFLAME, augment charge.
INGENIOUS, used indiscriminantly for ingenuous; intelligent, talented.
INGENUITY, ingenuousness.
INGENUOUS, generous.
INGINE. See Engin.
INGINER, engineer. (See Enginer).
INGLE, OR ENGHLE, bosom friend, intimate, minion.
INHABITABLE, uninhabitable.
INJURY, insult, affront.
IN-MATE, resident, indwelling.
INNATE, natural.

INNOCENT, simpleton.
INQUEST, jury, or other official body of inquiry.
INQUISITION, inquiry.
INSTANT, immediate.
INSTRUMENT, legal document.
INSURE, assure.
INTEGRATE, complete, perfect.
INTELLIGENCE, secret information, news.
INTEND, note carefully, attend, give ear to, be occupied with.
INTENDMENT, intention.
INTENT, intention, wish.
INTENTION, concentration of attention or gaze.
INTENTIVE, attentive.
INTERESSED, implicated.
INTRUDE, bring in forcibly or without leave.
INVINCIBLY, invisibly.
INWARD, intimate.
IRPE (uncertain), "a fantastic grimace, or contortion of the body: (Gifford)."
JACK, Jack o' the clock, automaton figure that strikes the hour; Jack-a-lent, puppet thrown at in Lent.
JACK, key of a virginal.
JACOB'S STAFF, an instrument for taking altitudes and distances.
JADE, befool.
JEALOUSY, JEALOUS, suspicion, suspicious.
JERKING, lashing.
JEW'S TRUMP, Jew's harp.
JIG, merry ballad or tune; a fanciful dialogue or light comic act introduced at the end or during an interlude of a play.
JOINED (JOINT)-STOOL, folding stool.
JOLL, jowl.
JOLTHEAD, blockhead.
JUMP, agree, tally.
JUST YEAR, no one was capable of the consulship until he was forty-three.
KELL, cocoon.
KELLY, an alchemist.
KEMB, comb.

KEMIA, vessel for distillation.
KIBE, chap, sore.
KILDERKIN, small barrel.
KILL, kiln.
KIND, nature; species; "do one's--," act according to one's nature.
KIRTLE, woman's gown of jacket and petticoat.
KISS OR DRINK AFORE ME, "this is a familiar expression, employed when what the speaker is just about to say is anticipated by another" (Gifford).
KIT, fiddle.
KNACK, snap, click.
KNIPPER-DOLING, a well-known Anabaptist.
KNITTING CUP, marriage cup.
KNOCKING, striking, weighty.
KNOT, company, band; a sandpiper or robin snipe (Tringa canutus); flower-bed laid out in fanciful design.
KURSINED, KYRSIN, christened.
LABOURED, wrought with labour and care.
LADE, load(ed).
LADING, load.
LAID, plotted.
LANCE-KNIGHT (Lanzknecht), a German mercenary foot-soldier.
LAP, fold.
LAR, household god.
LARD, garnish.
LARGE, abundant.
LARUM, alarum, call to arms.
LATTICE, tavern windows were furnished with lattices of various colours.
LAUNDER, to wash gold in aqua regia, so as imperceptibly to extract some of it.
LAVE, ladle, bale.
LAW, "give--," give a start (term of chase).
LAXATIVE, loose.
LAY ABOARD, run alongside generally with intent to board.
LEAGUER, siege, or camp of besieging army.
LEASING, lying.
LEAVE, leave off, desist.

LEER, leering or "empty, hence, perhaps, leer horse, a horse without a rider; leer is an adjective meaning uncontrolled, hence 'leer drunkards'" (Halliwell); according to Nares, a leer (empty) horse meant also a led horse; leeward, left.
LEESE, lose.
LEGS, "make--," do obeisance.
LEIGER, resident representative.
LEIGERITY, legerdemain.
LEMMA, subject proposed, or title of the epigram.
LENTER, slower.
LET, hinder.
LET, hindrance.
LEVEL COIL, a rough game...in which one hunted another from his seat. Hence used for any noisy riot (Halliwell).
LEWD, ignorant.
LEYSTALLS, receptacles of filth.
LIBERAL, ample.
LIEGER, ledger, register.
LIFT(ING), steal(ing); theft.
LIGHT, alight.
LIGHTLY, commonly, usually, often.
LIKE, please.
LIKELY, agreeable, pleasing.
LIME-HOUND, leash-, blood-hound.
LIMMER, vile, worthless.
LIN, leave off.
Line, "by--," by rule.
LINSTOCK, staff to stick in the ground, with forked head to hold a lighted match for firing cannon.
LIQUID, clear.
LIST, listen, hark; like, please.
LIVERY, legal term, delivery of the possession, etc.
LOGGET, small log, stick.
LOOSE, solution; upshot, issue; release of an arrow.
LOSE, give over, desist from; waste.
LOUTING, bowing, cringing.
LUCULENT, bright of beauty.
LUDGATHIANS, dealers on Ludgate Hill.

LURCH, rob, cheat.
LUTE, to close a vessel with some kind of cement.
MACK, unmeaning expletive.
MADGE-HOWLET or OWL, barn-owl.
MAIM, hurt, injury.
MAIN, chief concern (used as a quibble on heraldic term for "hand").
MAINPRISE, becoming surety for a prisoner so as to procure his release.
MAINTENANCE, giving aid, or abetting.
MAKE, mate.
MAKE, MADE, acquaint with business, prepare(d), instruct(ed).
MALLANDERS, disease of horses.
MALT HORSE, dray horse.
MAMMET, puppet.
MAMMOTHREPT, spoiled child.
MANAGE, control (term used for breaking-in horses); handling, administration.
MANGO, slave-dealer.
MANGONISE, polish up for sale.
MANIPLES, bundles, handfuls.
MANKIND, masculine, like a virago.
MANKIND, humanity.
MAPLE FACE, spotted face (N.E.D.).
MARCHPANE, a confection of almonds, sugar, etc.
MARK, "fly to the--," "generally said of a goshawk when, having 'put in' a covey of partridges, she takes stand, marking the spot where they disappeared from view until the falconer arrives to put them out to her" (Harting, Bibl. Accip. Gloss. 226).
MARLE, marvel.
MARROW-BONE MAN, one often on his knees for prayer.
MARRY! exclamation derived from the Virgin's name.
MARRY GIP, "probably originated from By Mary Gipcy" = St. Mary of Egypt, (N.E.D.).
MARTAGAN, Turk's cap lily.
MARYHINCHCO, stringhalt.
MASORETH, Masora, correct form of the scriptural text according to Hebrew tradition.
MASS, abb. for master.

MAUND, beg.
MAUTHER, girl, maid.
MEAN, moderation.
MEASURE, dance, more especially a stately one.
MEAT, "carry--in one's mouth," be a source of money or entertainment.
MEATH, metheglin.
MECHANICAL, belonging to mechanics, mean, vulgar.
MEDITERRANEO, middle aisle of St. Paul's, a general resort for business and amusement.
MEET WITH, even with.
MELICOTTON, a late kind of peach.
MENSTRUE, solvent.
MERCAT, market.
MERD, excrement.
MERE, undiluted; absolute, unmitigated.
MESS, party of four.
METHEGLIN, fermented liquor, of which one ingredient was honey.
METOPOSCOPY, study of physiognomy.
MIDDLING GOSSIP, go-between.
MIGNIARD, dainty, delicate.
MILE-END, training-ground of the city.
MINE-MEN, sappers.
MINION, form of cannon.
MINSITIVE, (?) mincing, affected (N.E.D.).
MISCELLANY MADAM, "a female trader in miscellaneous articles; a dealer in trinkets or ornaments of various kinds, such as kept shops in the New Exchange" (Nares).
MISCELLINE, mixed grain; medley.
MISCONCEIT, misconception.
MISPRISE, MISPRISION, mistake, misunderstanding.
MISTAKE AWAY, carry away as if by mistake.
MITHRIDATE, an antidote against poison.
MOCCINIGO, small Venetian coin, worth about ninepence.
MODERN, in the mode; ordinary, commonplace.
MOMENT, force or influence of value.
MONTANTO, upward stroke.
MONTH'S MIND, violent desire.

MOORISH, like a moor or waste.
MORGLAY, sword of Bevis of Southampton.
MORRICE-DANCE, dance on May Day, etc., in which certain personages were represented.
MORTALITY, death.
MORT-MAL, old sore, gangrene.
MOSCADINO, confection flavoured with musk.
MOTHER, Hysterica passio.
MOTION, proposal, request; puppet, puppet-show; "one of the small figures on the face of a large clock which was moved by the vibration of the pendulum" (Whalley).
MOTION, suggest, propose.
MOTLEY, parti-coloured dress of a fool; hence used to signify pertaining to, or like, a fool.
MOTTE, motto.
MOURNIVAL, set of four aces or court cards in a hand; a quartette.
MOW, setord hay or sheaves of grain.
MUCH! expressive of irony and incredulity.
MUCKINDER, handkerchief.
MULE, "born to ride on--," judges or serjeants-at-law formerly rode on mules when going in state to Westminster (Whally).
MULLETS, small pincers.
MUM-CHANCE, game of chance, played in silence.
MUN, must.
MUREY, dark crimson red.
MUSCOVY-GLASS, mica.
MUSE, wonder.
MUSICAL, in harmony.
MUSS, mouse; scramble.
MYROBOLANE, foreign conserve, "a dried plum, brought from the Indies."
MYSTERY, art, trade, profession.
NAIL, "to the--" (ad unguem), to perfection, to the very utmost.
NATIVE, natural.
NEAT, cattle.
NEAT, smartly apparelled; unmixed; dainty.
NEATLY, neatly finished.
NEATNESS, elegance.

NEIS, nose, scent.
NEUF (NEAF, NEIF), fist.
NEUFT, newt.
NIAISE, foolish, inexperienced person.
NICE, fastidious, trivial, finical, scrupulous.
NICENESS, fastidiousness.
NICK, exact amount; right moment; "set in the--," meaning uncertain.
NICE, suit, fit; hit, seize the right moment, etc., exactly hit on, hit off.
NOBLE, gold coin worth 6s. 8d.
NOCENT, harmful.
NIL, not will.
NOISE, company of musicians.
NOMENTACK, an Indian chief from Virginia.
NONES, nonce.
NOTABLE, egregious.
NOTE, sign, token.
NOUGHT, "be--," go to the devil, be hanged, etc.
NOWT-HEAD, blockhead.
NUMBER, rhythm.
NUPSON, oaf, simpleton.
OADE, woad.
OBARNI, preparation of mead.
OBJECT, oppose; expose; interpose.
OBLATRANT, barking, railing.
OBNOXIOUS, liable, exposed; offensive.
OBSERVANCE, homage, devoted service.
OBSERVANT, attentive, obsequious.
OBSERVE, show deference, respect.
OBSERVER, one who shows deference, or waits upon another.
OBSTANCY, legal phrase, "juridical opposition."
OBSTREPEROUS, clamorous, vociferous.
OBSTUPEFACT, stupefied.
ODLING, (?) "must have some relation to tricking and cheating" (Nares).
OMINOUS, deadly, fatal.
ONCE, at once; for good and all; used also for additional emphasis.
ONLY, pre-eminent, special.
OPEN, make public; expound.

OPPILATION, obstruction.
OPPONE, oppose.
OPPOSITE, antagonist.
OPPRESS, suppress.
ORIGINOUS, native.
ORT, remnant, scrap.
OUT, "to be--," to have forgotten one's part; not at one with each other.
OUTCRY, sale by auction.
OUTRECUIDANCE, arrogance, presumption.
OUTSPEAK, speak more than.
OVERPARTED, given too difficult a part to play.
OWLSPIEGEL. See Howleglass.
OYEZ! (O YES!), hear ye! call of the public crier when about to make a proclamation.
PACKING PENNY, "give a--," dismiss, send packing.
PAD, highway.
PAD-HORSE, road-horse.
PAINED (PANED) SLOPS, full breeches made of strips of different colour and material.
PAINFUL, diligent, painstaking.
PAINT, blush.
PALINODE, ode of recantation.
PALL, weaken, dim, make stale.
PALM, triumph.
PAN, skirt of dress or coat.
PANNEL, pad, or rough kind of saddle.
PANNIER-ALLY, inhabited by tripe-sellers.
PANNIER-MAN, hawker; a man employed about the inns of court to bring in provisions, set the table, etc.
PANTOFLE, indoor shoe, slipper.
PARAMENTOS, fine trappings.
PARANOMASIE, a play upon words.
PARANTORY, (?) peremptory.
PARCEL, particle, fragment (used contemptuously); article.
PARCEL, part, partly.
PARCEL-POET, poetaster.
PARERGA, subordinate matters.

PARGET, to paint or plaster the face.
PARLE, parley.
PARLOUS, clever, shrewd.
PART, apportion.
PARTAKE, participate in.
PARTED, endowed, talented.
PARTICULAR, individual person.
PARTIZAN, kind of halberd.
PARTRICH, partridge.
PARTS, qualities, endowments.
PASH, dash, smash.
PASS, care, trouble oneself.
PASSADO, fencing term: a thrust.
PASSAGE, game at dice.
PASSINGLY, exceedingly.
PASSION, effect caused by external agency.
PASSION, "in--," in so melancholy a tone, so pathetically.
PATOUN, (?) Fr. Paton, pellet of dough; perhaps the "moulding of the tobacco...for the pipe" (Gifford); (?) variant of Petun, South American name of tobacco.
PATRICO, the recorder, priest, orator of strolling beggars or gipsies.
PATTEN, shoe with wooden sole; "go--," keep step with, accompany.
PAUCA VERBA, few words.
PAVIN, a stately dance.
PEACE, "with my master's--," by leave, favour.
PECULIAR, individual, single.
PEDANT, teacher of the languages.
PEEL, baker's shovel.
PEEP, speak in a small or shrill voice.
PEEVISH(LY), foolish(ly), capricious(ly); childish(ly).
PELICAN, a retort fitted with tube or tubes, for continuous distillation.
PENCIL, small tuft of hair.
PERDUE, soldier accustomed to hazardous service.
PEREMPTORY, resolute, bold; imperious; thorough, utter, absolute(ly).
PERIMETER, circumference of a figure.
PERIOD, limit, end.
PERK, perk up.

PERPETUANA, "this seems to be that glossy kind of stuff now called everlasting, and anciently worn by serjeants and other city officers" (Gifford).
PERSPECTIVE, a view, scene or scenery; an optical device which gave a distortion to the picture unless seen from a particular point; a relief, modelled to produce an optical illusion.
PERSPICIL, optic glass.
PERSTRINGE, criticise, censure.
PERSUADE, inculcate, commend.
PERSWAY, mitigate.
PERTINACY, pertinacity.
PESTLING, pounding, pulverising, like a pestle.
PETASUS, broad-brimmed hat or winged cap worn by Mercury.
PETITIONARY, supplicatory.
PETRONEL, a kind of carbine or light gun carried by horsemen.
PETULANT, pert, insolent.
PHERE. See Fere.
PHLEGMA, watery distilled liquor (old chem. "water").
PHRENETIC, madman.
PICARDIL, stiff upright collar fastened on to the coat (Whalley).
PICT-HATCH, disreputable quarter of London.
PIECE, person, used for woman or girl; a gold coin worth in Jonson's time 20s. or 22s.
PIECES OF EIGHT, Spanish coin: piastre equal to eight reals.
PIED, variegated.
PIE-POUDRES (Fr. pied-poudreux, dusty-foot), court held at fairs to administer justice to itinerant vendors and buyers.
PILCHER, term of contempt; one who wore a buff or leather jerkin, as did the serjeants of the counter; a pilferer.
PILED, pilled, peeled, bald.
PILL'D, polled, fleeced.
PIMLICO, "sometimes spoken of as a person--perhaps master of a house famous for a particular ale" (Gifford).
PINE, afflict, distress.
PINK, stab with a weapon; pierce or cut in scallops for ornament.
PINNACE, a go-between in infamous sense.
PISMIRE, ant.
PISTOLET, gold coin, worth about 6s.

PITCH, height of a bird of prey's flight.
PLAGUE, punishment, torment.
PLAIN, lament.
PLAIN SONG, simple melody.
PLAISE, plaice.
PLANET, "struck with a--," planets were supposed to have powers of blasting or exercising secret influences.
PLAUSIBLE, pleasing.
PLAUSIBLY, approvingly.
PLOT, plan.
PLY, apply oneself to.
POESIE, posy, motto inside a ring.
POINT IN HIS DEVICE, exact in every particular.
POINTS, tagged laces or cords for fastening the breeches to the doublet.
POINT-TRUSSER, one who trussed (tied) his master's points (q.v.).
POISE, weigh, balance.
POKING-STICK, stick used for setting the plaits of ruffs.
POLITIC, politician.
POLITIC, judicious, prudent, political.
POLITICIAN, plotter, intriguer.
POLL, strip, plunder, gain by extortion.
POMANDER, ball of perfume, worn or hung about the person to prevent infection, or for foppery.
POMMADO, vaulting on a horse without the aid of stirrups.
PONTIC, sour.
POPULAR, vulgar, of the populace.
POPULOUS, numerous.
PORT, gate; print of a deer's foot.
PORT, transport.
PORTAGUE, Portuguese gold coin, worth over 3 or 4 pounds.
PORTCULLIS, "--of coin," some old coins have a portcullis stamped on their reverse (Whalley).
PORTENT, marvel, prodigy; sinister omen.
PORTENTOUS, prophesying evil, threatening.
PORTER, references appear "to allude to Parsons, the king's porter, who was...near seven feet high" (Whalley).
POSSESS, inform, acquaint.

POST AND PAIR, a game at cards.
POSY, motto. (See Poesie).
POTCH, poach.
POULT-FOOT, club-foot.
POUNCE, claw, talon.
PRACTICE, intrigue, concerted plot.
PRACTISE, plot, conspire.
PRAGMATIC, an expert, agent.
PRAGMATIC, officious, conceited, meddling.
PRECEDENT, record of proceedings.
PRECEPT, warrant, summons.
PRECISIAN(ISM), Puritan(ism), preciseness.
PREFER, recommend.
PRESENCE, presence chamber.
PRESENT(LY), immediate(ly), without delay; at the present time; actually.
PRESS, force into service.
PREST, ready.
PRETEND, assert, allege.
PREVENT, anticipate.
PRICE, worth, excellence.
PRICK, point, dot used in the writing of Hebrew and other languages.
PRICK, prick out, mark off, select; trace, track; "--away," make off with speed.
PRIMERO, game of cards.
PRINCOX, pert boy.
PRINT, "in--," to the letter, exactly.
PRISTINATE, former.
PRIVATE, private interests.
PRIVATE, privy, intimate.
PROCLIVE, prone to.
PRODIGIOUS, monstrous, unnatural.
PRODIGY, monster.
PRODUCED, prolonged.
PROFESS, pretend.
PROJECTION, the throwing of the "powder of projection" into the crucible to turn the melted metal into gold or silver.
PROLATE, pronounce drawlingly.

PROPER, of good appearance, handsome; own, particular.
PROPERTIES, stage necessaries.
PROPERTY, duty; tool.
PRORUMPED, burst out.
PROTEST, vow, proclaim (an affected word of that time); formally declare non-payment, etc., of bill of exchange; fig. failure of personal credit, etc.
PROVANT, soldier's allowance--hence, of common make.
PROVIDE, foresee.
PROVIDENCE, foresight, prudence.
PUBLICATION, making a thing public of common property (N.E.D.).
PUCKFIST, puff-ball; insipid, insignificant, boasting fellow.
PUFF-WING, shoulder puff.
PUISNE, judge of inferior rank, a junior.
PULCHRITUDE, beauty.
PUMP, shoe.
PUNGENT, piercing.
PUNTO, point, hit.
PURCEPT, precept, warrant.
PURE, fine, capital, excellent.
PURELY, perfectly, utterly.
PURL, pleat or fold of a ruff.
PURSE-NET, net of which the mouth is drawn together with a string.
PURSUIVANT, state messenger who summoned the persecuted seminaries; warrant officer.
PURSY, PURSINESS, shortwinded(ness).
PUT, make a push, exert yourself (N.E.D.).
PUT OFF, excuse, shift.
PUT ON, incite, encourage; proceed with, take in hand, try.
QUACKSALVER, quack.
QUAINT, elegant, elaborated, ingenious, clever.
QUAR, quarry.
QUARRIED, seized, or fed upon, as prey.
QUEAN, hussy, jade.
QUEASY, hazardous, delicate.
QUELL, kill, destroy.
QUEST, request; inquiry.
QUESTION, decision by force of arms.

QUESTMAN, one appointed to make official inquiry.
QUIB, QUIBLIN, quibble, quip.
QUICK, the living.
QUIDDIT, quiddity, legal subtlety.
QUIRK, clever turn or trick.
QUIT, requite, repay; acquit, absolve; rid; forsake, leave.
QUITTER-BONE, disease of horses.
QUODLING, codling.
QUOIT, throw like a quoit, chuck.
QUOTE, take note, observe, write down.
RACK, neck of mutton or pork (Halliwell).
RAKE UP, cover over.
RAMP, rear, as a lion, etc.
RAPT, carry away.
RAPT, enraptured.
RASCAL, young or inferior deer.
RASH, strike with a glancing oblique blow, as a boar with its tusk.
RATSEY, GOMALIEL, a famous highwayman.
RAVEN, devour.
REACH, understand.
REAL, regal.
REBATU, ruff, turned-down collar.
RECTOR, RECTRESS, director, governor.
REDARGUE, confute.
REDUCE, bring back.
REED, rede, counsel, advice.
REEL, run riot.
REFEL, refute.
REFORMADOES, disgraced or disbanded soldiers.
REGIMENT, government.
REGRESSION, return.
REGULAR ("Tale of a Tub"), regular noun (quibble) (N.E.D.).
RELIGION, "make--of," make a point of, scruple of.
RELISH, savour.
REMNANT, scrap of quotation.
REMORA, species of fish.
RENDER, depict, exhibit, show.
REPAIR, reinstate.

REPETITION, recital, narration.
REREMOUSE, bat.
RESIANT, resident.
RESIDENCE, sediment.
RESOLUTION, judgment, decision.
RESOLVE, inform; assure; prepare, make up one's mind; dissolve; come to a decision, be convinced; relax, set at ease.
RESPECTIVE, worthy of respect; regardful, discriminative.
RESPECTIVELY, with reverence.
RESPECTLESS, regardless.
RESPIRE, exhale; inhale.
RESPONSIBLE, correspondent.
REST, musket-rest.
REST, "set up one's--," venture one's all, one's last stake (from game of primero).
REST, arrest.
RESTIVE, RESTY, dull, inactive.
RETCHLESS(NESS), reckless(ness).
RETIRE, cause to retire.
RETRICATO, fencing term.
RETRIEVE, rediscovery of game once sprung.
RETURNS, ventures sent abroad, for the safe return of which so much money is received.
REVERBERATE, dissolve or blend by reflected heat.
REVERSE, REVERSO, back-handed thrust, etc., in fencing.
REVISE, reconsider a sentence.
RHEUM, spleen, caprice.
RIBIBE, abusive term for an old woman.
RID, destroy, do away with.
RIFLING, raffling, dicing.
RING, "cracked within the--," coins so cracked were unfit for currency.
RISSE, risen, rose.
RIVELLED, wrinkled.
ROARER, swaggerer.
ROCHET, fish of the gurnet kind.
ROCK, distaff.
RODOMONTADO, braggadocio.
ROGUE, vagrant, vagabond.

RONDEL, "a round mark in the score of a public-house" (Nares); roundel.
ROOK, sharper; fool, dupe.
ROSAKER, similar to ratsbane.
ROSA-SOLIS, a spiced spirituous liquor.
ROSES, rosettes.
ROUND, "gentlemen of the--," officers of inferior rank.
ROUND TRUNKS, trunk hose, short loose breeches reaching almost or quite to the knees.
ROUSE, carouse, bumper.
ROVER, arrow used for shooting at a random mark at uncertain distance.
ROWLY-POWLY, roly-poly.
RUDE, RUDENESS, unpolished, rough(ness), coarse(ness).
RUFFLE, flaunt, swagger.
RUG, coarse frieze.
RUG-GOWNS, gown made of rug.
RUSH, reference to rushes with which the floors were then strewn.
RUSHER, one who strewed the floor with rushes.
RUSSET, homespun cloth of neutral or reddish-brown colour.
SACK, loose, flowing gown.
SADLY, seriously, with gravity.
SAD(NESS), sober, serious(ness).
SAFFI, bailiffs.
ST. THOMAS A WATERINGS, place in Surrey where criminals were executed.
SAKER, small piece of ordnance.
SALT, leap.
SALT, lascivious.
SAMPSUCHINE, sweet marjoram.
SARABAND, a slow dance.
SATURNALS, began December 17.
SAUCINESS, presumption, insolence.
SAUCY, bold, impudent, wanton.
SAUNA (Lat.), a gesture of contempt.
SAVOUR, perceive; gratify, please; to partake of the nature.
SAY, sample.
SAY, assay, try.

SCALD, word of contempt, implying dirt and disease.
SCALLION, shalot, small onion.
SCANDERBAG, "name which the Turks (in allusion to Alexander the Great) gave to the brave Castriot, chief of Albania, with whom they had continual wars. His romantic life had just been translated" (Gifford).
SCAPE, escape.
SCARAB, beetle.
SCARTOCCIO, fold of paper, cover, cartouch, cartridge.
SCONCE, head.
SCOPE, aim.
SCOT AND LOT, tax, contribution (formerly a parish assessment).
SCOTOMY, dizziness in the head.
SCOUR, purge.
SCOURSE, deal, swap.
SCRATCHES, disease of horses.
SCROYLE, mean, rascally fellow.
SCRUPLE, doubt.
SEAL, put hand to the giving up of property or rights.
SEALED, stamped as genuine.
SEAM-RENT, ragged.
SEAMING LACES, insertion or edging.
SEAR UP, close by searing, burning.
SEARCED, sifted.
SECRETARY, able to keep a secret.
SECULAR, worldly, ordinary, commonplace.
SECURE, confident.
SEELIE, happy, blest.
SEISIN, legal term: possession.
SELLARY, lewd person.
SEMBLABLY, similarly.
SEMINARY, a Romish priest educated in a foreign seminary.
SENSELESS, insensible, without sense or feeling.
SENSIBLY, perceptibly.
SENSIVE, sensitive.
SENSUAL, pertaining to the physical or material.
SERENE, harmful dew of evening.
SERICON, red tincture.

SERVANT, lover.
SERVICES, doughty deeds of arms.
SESTERCE, Roman copper coin.
SET, stake, wager.
SET UP, drill.
SETS, deep plaits of the ruff.
SEWER, officer who served up the feast, and brought water for the hands of the guests.
SHAPE, a suit by way of disguise.
SHIFT, fraud, dodge.
SHIFTER, cheat.
SHITTLE, shuttle; "shittle-cock," shuttlecock.
SHOT, tavern reckoning.
SHOT-CLOG, one only tolerated because he paid the shot (reckoning) for the rest.
SHOT-FREE, scot-free, not having to pay.
SHOVE-GROAT, low kind of gambling amusement, perhaps somewhat of the nature of pitch and toss.
SHOT-SHARKS, drawers.
SHREWD, mischievous, malicious, curst.
SHREWDLY, keenly, in a high degree.
SHRIVE, sheriff; posts were set up before his door for proclamations, or to indicate his residence.
SHROVING, Shrovetide, season of merriment.
SIGILLA, seal, mark.
SILENCED BRETHERN, MINISTERS, those of the Church or Nonconformists who had been silenced, deprived, etc.
SILLY, simple, harmless.
SIMPLE, silly, witless; plain, true.
SIMPLES, herbs.
SINGLE, term of chase, signifying when the hunted stag is separated from the herd, or forced to break covert.
SINGLE, weak, silly.
SINGLE-MONEY, small change.
SINGULAR, unique, supreme.
SI-QUIS, bill, advertisement.
SKELDRING, getting money under false pretences; swindling.
SKILL, "it--s not," matters not.

SKINK(ER), pour, draw(er), tapster.
SKIRT, tail.
SLEEK, smooth.
SLICE, fire shovel or pan (dial.).
SLICK, sleek, smooth.
'SLID, 'SLIGHT, 'SPRECIOUS, irreverent oaths.
SLIGHT, sleight, cunning, cleverness; trick.
SLIP, counterfeit coin, bastard.
SLIPPERY, polished and shining.
SLOPS, large loose breeches.
SLOT, print of a stag's foot.
SLUR, put a slur on; cheat (by sliding a die in some way).
SMELT, gull, simpleton.
SNORLE, "perhaps snarl, as Puppy is addressed" (Cunningham).
SNOTTERIE, filth.
SNUFF, anger, resentment; "take in--," take offence at.
SNUFFERS, small open silver dishes for holding snuff, or receptacle for placing snuffers in (Halliwell).
SOCK, shoe worn by comic actors.
SOD, seethe.
SOGGY, soaked, sodden.
SOIL, "take--," said of a hunted stag when he takes to the water for safety.
SOL, sou.
SOLDADOES, soldiers.
SOLICIT, rouse, excite to action.
SOOTH, flattery, cajolery.
SOOTHE, flatter, humour.
SOPHISTICATE, adulterate.
SORT, company, party; rank, degree.
SORT, suit, fit; select.
SOUSE, ear.
SOUSED ("Devil is an Ass"), fol. read "sou't," which Dyce interprets as "a variety of the spelling of "shu'd": to "shu" is to scare a bird away." (See his "Webster," page 350).
SOWTER, cobbler.
SPAGYRICA, chemistry according to the teachings of Paracelsus.
SPAR, bar.

SPEAK, make known, proclaim.
SPECULATION, power of sight.
SPED, to have fared well, prospered.
SPEECE, species.
SPIGHT, anger, rancour.
SPINNER, spider.
SPINSTRY, lewd person.
SPITTLE, hospital, lazar-house.
SPLEEN, considered the seat of the emotions.
SPLEEN, caprice, humour, mood.
SPRUNT, spruce.
SPURGE, foam.
SPUR-RYAL, gold coin worth 15s.
SQUIRE, square, measure; "by the--," exactly.
STAGGERING, wavering, hesitating.
STAIN, disparagement, disgrace.
STALE, decoy, or cover, stalking-horse.
STALE, make cheap, common.
STALK, approach stealthily or under cover.
STALL, forestall.
STANDARD, suit.
STAPLE, market, emporium.
STARK, downright.
STARTING-HOLES, loopholes of escape.
STATE, dignity; canopied chair of state; estate.
STATUMINATE, support vines by poles or stakes; used by Pliny (Gifford).
STAY, gag.
STAY, await; detain.
STICKLER, second or umpire.
STIGMATISE, mark, brand.
STILL, continual(ly), constant(ly).
STINKARD, stinking fellow.
STINT, stop.
STIPTIC, astringent.
STOCCATA, thrust in fencing.
STOCK-FISH, salted and dried fish.
STOMACH, pride, valour.

STOMACH, resent.
STOOP, swoop down as a hawk.
STOP, fill, stuff.
STOPPLE, stopper.
STOTE, stoat, weasel.
STOUP, stoop, swoop=bow.
STRAIGHT, straightway.
STRAMAZOUN (Ital. stramazzone), a down blow, as opposed to the thrust.
STRANGE, like a stranger, unfamiliar.
STRANGENESS, distance of behaviour.
STREIGHTS, OR BERMUDAS, labyrinth of alleys and courts in the Strand.
STRIGONIUM, Grau in Hungary, taken from the Turks in 1597.
STRIKE, balance (accounts).
STRINGHALT, disease of horses.
STROKER, smoother, flatterer.
STROOK, p.p. of "strike."
STRUMMEL-PATCHED, strummel is glossed in dialect dicts. as "a long, loose and dishevelled head of hair."
STUDIES, studious efforts.
STYLE, title; pointed instrument used for writing on wax tablets.
SUBTLE, fine, delicate, thin; smooth, soft.
SUBTLETY (SUBTILITY), subtle device.
SUBURB, connected with loose living.
SUCCUBAE, demons in form of women.
SUCK, extract money from.
SUFFERANCE, suffering.
SUMMED, term of falconry: with full-grown plumage.
SUPER-NEGULUM, topers turned the cup bottom up when it was empty.
SUPERSTITIOUS, over-scrupulous.
SUPPLE, to make pliant.
SURBATE, make sore with walking.
SURCEASE, cease.
SUR-REVERENCE, save your reverence.
SURVISE, peruse.
SUSCITABILITY, excitability.

SUSPECT, suspicion.
SUSPEND, suspect.
SUSPENDED, held over for the present.
SUTLER, victualler.
SWAD, clown, boor.
SWATH BANDS, swaddling clothes.
SWINGE, beat.
TABERD, emblazoned mantle or tunic worn by knights and heralds.
TABLE(S), "pair of--," tablets, note-book.
TABOR, small drum.
TABRET, tabor.
TAFFETA, silk; "tuft-taffeta," a more costly silken fabric.
TAINT, "--a staff," break a lance at tilting in an unscientific or dishonourable manner.
TAKE IN, capture, subdue.
TAKE ME WITH YOU, let me understand you.
TAKE UP, obtain on credit, borrow.
TALENT, sum or weight of Greek currency.
TALL, stout, brave.
TANKARD-BEARERS, men employed to fetch water from the conduits.
TARLETON, celebrated comedian and jester.
TARTAROUS, like a Tartar.
TAVERN-TOKEN, "to swallow a--," get drunk.
TELL, count.
TELL-TROTH, truth-teller.
TEMPER, modify, soften.
TENDER, show regard, care for, cherish; manifest.
TENT, "take--," take heed.
TERSE, swept and polished.
TERTIA, "that portion of an army levied out of one particular district or division of a country" (Gifford).
TESTON, tester, coin worth 6d.
THIRDBOROUGH, constable.
THREAD, quality.
THREAVES, droves.
THREE-FARTHINGS, piece of silver current under Elizabeth.
THREE-PILED, of finest quality, exaggerated.
THRIFTILY, carefully.

THRUMS, ends of the weaver's warp; coarse yarn made from.
THUMB-RING, familiar spirits were supposed capable of being carried about in various ornaments or parts of dress.
TIBICINE, player on the tibia, or pipe.
TICK-TACK, game similar to backgammon.
TIGHTLY, promptly.
TIM, (?) expressive of a climax of nonentity.
TIMELESS, untimely, unseasonable.
TINCTURE, an essential or spiritual principle supposed by alchemists to be transfusible into material things; an imparted characteristic or tendency.
TINK, tinkle.
TIPPET, "turn--," change behaviour or way of life.
TIPSTAFF, staff tipped with metal.
TIRE, head-dress.
TIRE, feed ravenously, like a bird of prey.
TITILLATION, that which tickles the senses, as a perfume.
TOD, fox.
TOILED, worn out, harassed.
TOKEN, piece of base metal used in place of very small coin, when this was scarce.
TONNELS, nostrils.
TOP, "parish--," large top kept in villages for amusement and exercise in frosty weather when people were out of work.
TOTER, tooter, player on a wind instrument.
TOUSE, pull, rend.
TOWARD, docile, apt; on the way to; as regards; present, at hand.
TOY, whim; trick; term of contempt.
TRACT, attraction.
TRAIN, allure, entice.
TRANSITORY, transmittable.
TRANSLATE, transform.
TRAY-TRIP, game at dice (success depended on throwing a three) (Nares).
TREACHOUR (TRECHER), traitor.
TREEN, wooden.
TRENCHER, serving-man who carved or served food.
TRENDLE-TAIL, trundle-tail, curly-tailed.

TRICK (TRICKING), term of heraldry: to draw outline of coat of arms, etc., without blazoning.

TRIG, a spruce, dandified man.

TRILL, trickle.

TRILLIBUB, tripe, any worthless, trifling thing.

TRIPOLY, "come from--," able to perform feats of agility, a "jest nominal," depending on the first part of the word (Gifford).

TRITE, worn, shabby.

TRIVIA, three-faced goddess (Hecate).

TROJAN, familiar term for an equal or inferior; thief.

TROLL, sing loudly.

TROMP, trump, deceive.

TROPE, figure of speech.

TROW, think, believe, wonder.

TROWLE, troll.

TROWSES, breeches, drawers.

TRUCHMAN, interpreter.

TRUNDLE, JOHN, well-known printer.

TRUNDLE, roll, go rolling along.

TRUNDLING CHEATS, term among gipsies and beggars for carts or coaches (Gifford).

TRUNK, speaking-tube.

TRUSS, tie the tagged laces that fastened the breeches to the doublet.

TUBICINE, trumpeter.

TUCKET (Ital. toccato), introductory flourish on the trumpet.

TUITION, guardianship.

TUMBLER, a particular kind of dog so called from the mode of his hunting.

TUMBREL-SLOP, loose, baggy breeches.

TURD, excrement.

TUSK, gnash the teeth (Century Dict.).

TWIRE, peep, twinkle.

TWOPENNY ROOM, gallery.

TYRING-HOUSE, attiring-room.

ULENSPIEGEL. See Howleglass.

UMBRATILE, like or pertaining to a shadow.

UMBRE, brown dye.

UNBATED, unabated.

UNBORED, (?) excessively bored.
UNCARNATE, not fleshly, or of flesh.
UNCOUTH, strange, unusual.
UNDERTAKER, "one who undertook by his influence in the House of Commons to carry things agreeably to his Majesty's wishes" (Whalley); one who becomes surety for.
UNEQUAL, unjust.
UNEXCEPTED, no objection taken at.
UNFEARED, unaffrighted.
UNHAPPILY, unfortunately.
UNICORN'S HORN, supposed antidote to poison.
UNKIND(LY), unnatural(ly).
UNMANNED, untamed (term in falconry).
UNQUIT, undischarged.
UNREADY, undressed.
UNRUDE, rude to an extreme.
UNSEASONED, unseasonable, unripe.
UNSEELED, a hawk's eyes were "seeled" by sewing the eyelids together with fine thread.
UNTIMELY, unseasonably.
UNVALUABLE, invaluable.
UPBRAID, make a matter of reproach.
UPSEE, heavy kind of Dutch beer (Halliwell); "--Dutch," in the Dutch fashion.
UPTAILS ALL, refrain of a popular song.
URGE, allege as accomplice, instigator.
URSHIN, URCHIN, hedgehog.
USE, interest on money; part of sermon dealing with the practical application of doctrine.
USE, be in the habit of, accustomed to; put out to interest.
USQUEBAUGH, whisky.
USURE, usury.
UTTER, put in circulation, make to pass current; put forth for sale.
VAIL, bow, do homage.
VAILS, tips, gratuities.
VALL. See Vail.
VALLIES (Fr. valise), portmanteau, bag.

VAPOUR(S) (n. and v.), used affectedly, like "humour," in many senses, often very vaguely and freely ridiculed by Jonson; humour, disposition, whims, brag(ging), hector(ing), etc.

VARLET, bailiff, or serjeant-at-mace.

VAUT, vault.

VEER (naut.), pay out.

VEGETAL, vegetable; person full of life and vigour.

VELLUTE, velvet.

VELVET CUSTARD. Cf. "Taming of the Shrew," iv. 3, 82, "custard coffin," coffin being the raised crust over a pie.

VENT, vend, sell; give outlet to; scent, snuff up.

VENUE, bout (fencing term).

VERDUGO (Span.), hangman, executioner.

VERGE, "in the--," within a certain distance of the court.

VEX, agitate, torment.

VICE, the buffoon of old moralities; some kind of machinery for moving a puppet (Gifford).

VIE AND REVIE, to hazard a certain sum, and to cover it with a larger one.

VINCENT AGAINST YORK, two heralds-at-arms.

VINDICATE, avenge.

VIRGE, wand, rod.

VIRGINAL, old form of piano.

VIRTUE, valour.

VIVELY, in lifelike manner, livelily.

VIZARD, mask.

VOGUE, rumour, gossip.

VOICE, vote.

VOID, leave, quit.

VOLARY, cage, aviary.

VOLLEY, "at--," "o' the volee," at random (from a term of tennis).

VORLOFFE, furlough.

WADLOE, keeper of the Devil Tavern, where Jonson and his friends met in the 'Apollo' room (Whalley).

WAIGHTS, waits, night musicians, "band of musical watchmen" (Webster), or old form of "hautboys."

WANNION, "vengeance," "plague" (Nares).

WARD, a famous pirate.

WARD, guard in fencing.
WATCHET, pale, sky blue.
WEAL, welfare.
WEED, garment.
WEFT, waif.
WEIGHTS, "to the gold--," to every minute particular.
WELKIN, sky.
WELL-SPOKEN, of fair speech.
WELL-TORNED, turned and polished, as on a wheel.
WELT, hem, border of fur.
WHER, whether.
WHETSTONE, GEORGE, an author who lived 1544(?) to 1587(?).
WHIFF, a smoke, or drink; "taking the--," inhaling the tobacco smoke or some such accomplishment.
WHIGH-HIES, neighings, whinnyings.
WHIMSY, whim, "humour."
WHINILING, (?) whining, weakly.
WHIT, (?) a mere jot.
WHITEMEAT, food made of milk or eggs.
WICKED, bad, clumsy.
WICKER, pliant, agile.
WILDING, esp. fruit of wild apple or crab tree (Webster).
WINE, "I have the--for you," Prov.: I have the perquisites (of the office) which you are to share (Cunningham).
WINNY, "same as old word "wonne," to stay, etc." (Whalley).
WISE-WOMAN, fortune-teller.
WISH, recommend.
WISS (WUSSE), "I--," certainly, of a truth.
WITHOUT, beyond.
WITTY, cunning, ingenious, clever.
WOOD, collection, lot.
WOODCOCK, term of contempt.
WOOLSACK ("--pies"), name of tavern.
WORT, unfermented beer.
WOUNDY, great, extreme.
WREAK, revenge.
WROUGHT, wrought upon.
WUSSE, interjection. (See Wiss).

YEANLING, lamb, kid.
ZANY, an inferior clown, who attended upon the chief fool and mimicked his tricks.